Evans.

Continuum

Continuum. A progression of elements varying by minute degrees—
Webster's Dictionary
Suzanne Evans.

Continuum

Suzanne Evans

SterlingHouse
Pittsburgh, PA

Sterling House
PUBLISHER

ISBN 1-156315-111-1

Mass Market Paperback

First Printing—1998

Request for information should be addressed to:

Sterling House Publisher
The Sterling Building
440 Friday Road
Department T-101
Pittsburgh, PA 15209

Cover design & Typesetting: Drawing Board Studios

Library Of Congress Number
97-06407

Printed in the United States of America

Dedication

To the three men in my life, my mother, and my family

&

To the women in crises

Acknowledgment

There are many people who have supported me in my goal to have published *Continuum*. The many days Gail and I spent formulating the storyline of *Continuum* is something I will treasure forever. To Cindi Sterling of the Lee Shore Literary Agency who answered the telephone one Friday afternoon more than three years ago, it is a moment I will never forget. It made me realize that I have a lot to learn about writing a book. I appreciated the time that she took to focus my ambition. SterlingHouse Publisher has been most supportive and I am grateful. The patience of Michele Burton-Brown, Managing Editor is limitless. Finally the editorial comments of Melanie Hinkle, Assistant Editor put the needed finishing touches to the book.

Prologue

Marni Taylor watched as a flock of birds gracefully swooped down in single file, their claws firmly grasping the wide rim of the birdbath. The spray of water from the fountain coated their bodies, leaving their feathers glistening in the sunlight. In unison they dipped their beaks into the water. It was eight o'clock Tuesday morning; the thermometer nailed to the window frame showed the mercury at ninety degrees. Marni continued to watch the birds fly through the cascading water, and every so often stop to rest. The simplistic scene soothed her, allowing the comfort of a few tranquil moments, the calm before the storm. Then like so often in the past few months, a kaleidoscope of her married life flashed through her mind. One second she was seeing Don propose marriage to her. Next, they were dancing at their wedding. She was driving to the hospital for the birth of her first son. The scene was repeated but this time she gave birth to her younger son. The image of the local banker appeared. He was helping Don and her finalize mortgage documents for the purchase of their house, the house they now called home. Of all the familiar images, the last prompted a flux of emotions. She hoped the frustration, the anger and the disappointment she harbored would all go away when she signed the divorce papers ending sixteen years of marriage. Something she should have initiated years ago.

Yesterday Marni was on the telephone with Alan Davidson discussing the sale of his property. It was about the relevancy of a new zoning regulation allowing mansions to be converted into multiple dwellings. Suddenly a bolt of lightning struck her. Why did Don have to be the one to move out? Why couldn't she do the moving? Marni quickly ended her phone conversation with Alan, promising to call him back later in the day. Wasting no time she punched numbers into her calculator. It wasn't long before she saw with two partners, she could purchase Alan's estate.

Her years of experience as a North Shore real estate broker made her an expert on such property. The development potential for a mansion sitting on six acres of waterfront property was limitless. The new regulation launched Alan's estate into a marketable entity. There would be a new group of investors knocking on her office door to inspect the property. If she wanted it, she would have to move quickly. For the past twelve months Marni had been showing the estate at least once a week. She started the tour of the estate by parking at the exact place where she could show off the magnificence of the house. Blindfolded, she could walk through each room pointing to the finest architectural features. She fantasized with every customer how best to decorate the house to satisfy their tastes. Each time the fateful moment arose to put their name on the dotted line, the potential buyer backed out, afraid the estate would become a money pit.

With the purchase proposal Marni drew up, the estate became affordable. The mansion was divided into three luxury residences, leaving the main level and the exterior premises to be owned and used by each partner. Marni didn't care who her neighbors were. She wanted to concentrate on closing the deal and putting together a twosome where the odds were in her favor to sell the investment.

Kimberly and Nina immediately became her candidates. They were currently looking for new homes and in a price range comparable to a share in the estate. She had found them their present homes. During the stress of house hunting they had remained friendly and cooperative. Disregarding her rule of not socializing with clients, occasionally she went to dinner with each woman. Therefore, Marni didn't hesitate to make an appointment with them for today. On the ride over to the estate she planned to give the women background information on the property and discuss her proposal. They were in a financial position to invest and she had faith in her ability to convince them it was a right move. There was a reason the sign 'Martay Real Estate' hung outside the building that she owned.

Marni thought about Kimberly Mathews. She had to move because her lease was up in four months. Marni knew that was a big plus. She also felt a bond existed between her and Kimberly.

They discussed their involvement in professional careers, parenting and the state of the real estate market. Kimberly, like Marni was very industrious busily promoting and developing her own firm, Mathews Architectural Group and earning a very fine reputation. Marni knew that for a fact; they had common clients. It was Marni who said of herself she was a trapeze artist. Carefully, she balanced her time so she could have a career and still have quality time with her children. She knew Kimberly thought the same way. Kimberly was always punctual when they had an appointment. Again Marni mentally put a check mark to Kimberly's name.

Nina Levin was also a perfect candidate. Her present home was sold and scheduled to close in three months, and because of this, Nina would be motivated to join the investment. She would bring a certain distinction to the deal. Nina was a celebrated painter. Her abstract works of art hung in museums and galleries all over the world. Marni compared Nina to a musical director. The conductor used his bantam in a concert hall to bring together the musicians. Nina used a brush on a canvas to orchestrate her strokes, color and shapes into an exciting piece of artwork. Marni saw something new every time she looked at Nina's abstract hanging on her living room wall. When others admired the painting, she liked telling them that she knew the artist personally. Marni always looked forward to spending time with Nina. She was deeply drawn to an aura about Nina—her free spirit and sense of elan vital. It was contagious.

Marnie glanced out the window. She noted in disappointment that the birdbath was deserted. She looked at her watch and realized, with a start, that her daydreaming had cost her precious time. The two women would be arriving in one hour. She walked to her desk and began reviewing the paperwork she would pass out during the car ride. Then for the thousandth time she skimmed her notes on the oral presentation.

A knock on the door interrupted her concentration.

"Come in," Marni called to Ellen, her office manager.

"Just reminding you," Ellen said, peering into the office, "fifteen minutes until show time."

"Thanks Ellen. I was just about to gather my things."

Five minutes later Marni stood alongside her car in the parking lot. She chauffeured her clients in a 1959 white El Dorado convertible. Since the weather permitted, the canvas top was down. She suspected the clients liked the mode of transportation. Marni waited for the women's cars to enter the parking lot.

Kimberly driving her 300SL silver Mercedes pulled into the empty space next to Marni's car. It was exactly 10:00 A.M. Marni wasn't surprised. Kimberly stepped out of her car perfectly dressed for success and Marni believed the envy of many women. Her long blond hair and statuesque body looked particularly outstanding today in a Channel-styled white linen suit.

"Hi, Kimberly," Marni said as the woman approached her.

"Great weather to see some property," Kimberly replied.

"Nina should be coming along shortly." Within seconds of Marni's statement, she heard a car door slam shut. Marni looked over her shoulder. "Here she is." She announced to Kimberly,

Nina was hopping around the parked cars. Her full-bosomed chest bounced beneath a sheer jungle print tunic partially covering a brown leather miniskirt. The alligator boots, warm for today's weather, went as high as the calf of her leg, and a matching alligator pouch hung from her shoulder. Around her neck she wore a gold chain necklace with oversized links, and matching links dangled from her ears. Her chestnut hair was outrageously teased and hung in a wild mane around her shoulder. She was waving her left hand while clutching a wide-brimmed straw hat. Marni chuckled to herself, thinking she wouldn't be caught dead in such an outfit. Now that both women arrived, Marni lifted her hand toward Kimberly and said, "Kimberly Mathews, meet Nina Levin." She repeated the motion in Nina's direction. "Nina Levin, meet Kimberly Mathews." Exchanging hand shakes, the women said, "Hello." In a cheery voice Nina said to Marni, "We're ready for the showing." Then Nina gently shoved Kimberly with her hip. Marni noticed the overture surprised Kimberly but Marni picked up on Nina's anxiousness and immediately opened the car door. She held the front seat forward while the two women maneuvered themselves into the back of car finally sitting with a white leather armrest between them. Within seconds Marni eased her slender body behind the wheel. She pushed a button to adapt her height of five feet four inches into a comfortable sitting position. Before buckling her safety belt she smoothed out her khaki suit jacket and short skirt. With her right hand, she tucked her straight black hair behind her ears. It revealed more of her perfect features—large brown almond shaped eyes, high cheek bones, a small straight nose and lips perfectly suited to her rounded chin. "All set," she said turning her head. She flashed Kimberly and Nina a smile. Then she started the car. Driving out of the parking lot, Marni turned onto Northern Boulevard. She had several miles to drive on the county road. Kimberly and Nina were chatting about neutral topics of weather and traffic. Again Marni smoothed her hair, a habit of hers before initiating a sale's pitch. Routinely, she moved her paperwork closer to her. Looking into the rear view mirror Marni interrupted the women's conversation. "Thanks for coordinating your schedules with only twenty-four hours notice," she said.

"Forget it," Nina responded quickly.

"Oh, I know it had to be difficult for you. A cesspool problem is no picnic."

"Too bad," Kimberly said softly.

Marni glanced in Kimberly's direction. She decided Kimberly's facial expression showed concern. Marni intended to cause a cohesive feeling between the two women. Her strategy was working. "Nina, you're a martyr," Marni said. "Yesterday you sounded agitated on the phone. Fill us in."

"If you must know," Nina bellowed, "what pissed me off is that I can't work. The backup has flooded my studio. What a mess! I had to leave my mop to keep this appointment."

"That's a bummer," Marni said.

"Not to mention the smell!" Nina exclaimed.

"I can sympathize," Marni said. "The smell does eventually go away. When it happened in my house, I couldn't believe it.

For days after I walked from room to room, spraying perfumed."

"I hope, you don't mind me asking," Kimberly said in her usual soft tone, "but are you sure you need to replace the cesspool?"

"Unfortunately, yes," Nina answered. "The house is very old but everything must work when I sign the closing documents. Right Marni?" Marni nodded. Then realizing Nina's capriciousness, she added, "Let's not mess up the deal. You wanted to sell the house and I got you a buyer, didn't I?"

"Just kidding," Nina said lowering her eyes. "Just kidding."

"Would you like me to recommend a plumber?" Kimberly asked Nina. Her voice sounding more assertive than a few moments ago. "My firm has a good working relationship with many contractors."

"Thanks, but I've one all lined up," Nina answered. Looking up, she placed her palms together. "I hope!"

"In case you run into a problem, please call me," Kimberly said. "I can help you." She slipped her business card into Nina's handbag on the armrest. Marni was pleased with the interaction between the two women. They were establishing a relationship. The first phase of her strategy worked successfully. She was ready to roll up her sleeves and sell, sell and sell.

"Now let's turn our thoughts to the reason I asked for this appointment," Marni said to the two women. "We're all looking for a new place to live. There's an opportunity to participate together." Marni sensed the women's eyes were focused on her. "I have a unique property to show you." She passed back to them a rendering of the property. Kimberly did what Marni expected an architect to do. Silently, she studied the rendering. Nina had a different response. She glanced quickly at the rendering. Wildly, she shook the paper in the air. "Hurry up and tell us all you know about this property," she urged.

"That's just what I plan to do," Marni replied calmly. Her timing was perfect. She had just entered the prestigious North Shore community where the estate was located. The enclave was part of the gold coast of Long Island. Large homesites were constructed so the property lines included beach frontage of Long Island Sound or a water view. "The estate," Marni began, "was built by a prominent banking family in the late 1930's. Some family member lived there until the 1960's, since then it was sold several times, each owner sustained the life style of grandeur. The facade of the estate house is the epitome of elegance. It stayed virtually intact except a few necessary electrical and plumbing upgrades. Then there was the usual face lifting such as painting the trim and sandblasting the red brick surface. You'll see, it's an imposing structure surrounded by six very choice acres. In my proposal the grounds are a common area for all of us to own and use," Marni said turning around. "There is much to enjoy. The amenities include frontage on the Sound, a sandy beach area, a dock for small craft and even a charming guesthouse. If either of you like to do laps, there's a heated olympic-size swimming pool."

"It sounds really nifty," Nina said.

"Kimberly, I know you're a great tennis player," Marni said. "How about playing on your own court?"

"A tennis court," Kimberly said. "I'd like that. It'll save traveling time to my weekly games. Time is precious to me."

Marni felt positive vibrations coming from each woman. She continued to drive slowly through the quiet streets. "Every house has a story," Marni said. "For instance there's the Hughes," Marni said, pointing her finger at a Tudor-styled house. "I'm sure you have heard about them. They donated one million dollars in their son's memory for the research and cure of AIDS. It was in the newspaper." Marni shook her head. "AIDS is always such a sad story. For the Hughes their son's death was more tragic. He was an only child."

"It's sad what happens to families," Nina responded softly.

Marni chauffeured the women passed velvet green lawns, stone pillars, cobblestone driveways and multi-winged mansions. "One pretty setting after another," Nina said. "Wait until you see the Davidson estate," Marni said. "I think it tops them all. The rolling green lawn is filled with a variety of planting-white, purple and pink rhododendrons, sculptured evergreens perfectly trimmed and many colorful flower beds."

"It sounds like so much upkeep," Kimberly said. She knew the kind of responsibility involved maintaining large grounds. Her commercial buildings and residential deluxe homes were such that she always consulted with landscape designers. The concern was mixing low maintenance shrubbery with specimen planting to keep the labor problem under control.

"Think of it as our own park," Nina said to Kimberly as she reassuringly pattered her arm.

"Don't worry Kimberly," Marni said. "We'll have a gardener," Marni continued with her pitch. "The mansion is large enough to have three residences, one for each of us." For a few minutes she was silent, allowing the women to study the layout detailed on the rendering. Marni, feeling the timing right, picked up the paperwork laying next to her and passed it to the women. "Please look over the proposal. The numbers speak for themselves." She watched the women through the mirror carefully review the pages. She knew that these women were accustomed to analyzing financial statistics. It was one reason for their success. They would now make their decision because the numbers made sense. Pressure to find a new home supported a decision to go forward. Marni's intuition told her they would become partners despite the women's visible differences.

"The numbers seem good to me," Kimberly said looking up. She did a similar kind of analysis before making a decision to do a project. "I'll consider the investment although I still have some doubts."

"Me," Nina said leaning forward and squeezing Marni's shoulder, "I'm a captive audience. Keep your foot on the pedal."

"Aye, aye, Madam," Marni replied happily.

Marni pulled up to a wrought-iron gate and stopped the car. Mounted across the black iron was a brightly polished brass plate bearing the inscription SOUNDVIEW 1933. It was flanked on either side by a ten-foot-tall wall.

"I'm glad, we're in this neighborhood," Nina said. "It's by far my favorite."

Pushing the intercom button, Marni identified herself. The gate swung open. Marni drove the car along the now familiar driveway and again she felt protected passing beneath the sentry-like pines lining the road. She steered the car slowly, controlling her anticipated excitement, knowing as she moved around the curve, the mansion would be before the women's eyes.

"Amazing," Nina said.

"Perfect," Kimberly said.

Marni stopped the car reaching her usual spot and allowed Kimberly and Nina to enjoy the spectacular view of the mansion. The regal home was a marvel of French architecture and red brick masonry. Long rectangular stone quoins distinguished each corner, embellishing the strength of the mansions. A mansard roof was made of dark gray shingles, and gable windows were carefully placed to run across the roof's lower slope. Keeping with the French tradition, each window was enhanced by a white cornice ornamented with dentils. Brass carriage lights highlighted the impressive double-door entry.

"Let's get out of the car for a few minutes," Marni suggested. "Take the rendering with you." Marni led the women toward a pond filled with floating lilies and fish flitting beneath water. "Isn't this charming?" Nina said leaning over the pond's edge to get a better look. "A good place to set up my easel." Marni liked that idea. "I have another place for your easel, Nina, follow me," she said. She led the women to a wooden bridge mounted across the center of the pond. Silently, Marni watched Kimberly and Nina gaze at the estate on its impeccably manicured lawn. She thought that it was just as she described with one exception: it was ablaze by the powerful light of noon sunbeams. "A storybook setting," Marni said softly.

"Don't you think?"

"It's more than that," Nina said realizing it resembled Pierre's chateau, her magic kingdom, and still her favorite place in all the world. She closed her eyes and felt his hands caress her face, her heartbeat quickened. Spontaneously, she reached up to return the loving touch but it was only air. Fifteen years ago she left Paris but she was still under his spell.

"Anything wrong Nina?" Marni asked.

"No, no, just swatting a fly."

"I wish the estate were far away on another planet," Kimberly whispered. A place where George could never find her or Candy. She knew that wasn't likely. Possibly, she thought, Soundview, could provide the refuge needed for a new start.

"Tell me," Nina said, "before I burst. "Is that the artist studio?" She lifted her arm and pointed her fingers to the left wing. The third floor resembled a greenhouse.

"That's it," Marni said. "It has a panoramic view of Long Island Sound and the estate grounds. The studio should get your creative juices flowing."

"I'd like that," Nina said excitedly. Her work had been flat lately, lacking the excitement that radiated from her canvases. She missed Marty. They worked in the studio together. He did his sculpting and she did her painting. Now there was emptiness. She hadn't heard from him since he began his apprenticeship. She pressured him to get on with his career though she knew that she'd feel the loss.

"Look at the distance between the front doors," Marni said. Although they would be sharing the mansion at a cost equal to ownership of a private house, they weren't compromising their privacy of their individuality. "Each wing has a front door and back door leading to the outside," Marni explained. "There's no inside access to the main house. The past owners of Soundview had their privacy and you'll have yours." Marni wanted Nina and Kimberly to be assured of this.

Nina approximated the distance between wings and the main structure in the center and quickly decided that it would work for her. If she had visitors they could pull right up to her door and avoid scrutiny. Her personal life was her own business. "It seems private to me," Nina said. "I'm ready for the house tour."

Marni knew that she had one partner. Kimberly, she thought, would be more difficult.

"I'm more concerned with the security devices," Kimberly said.

"No one can enter without being announced," Marni said. "The entire mansion is wired, too."

"That's good," Kimberly replied. She hoped that this would keep Candy safe from her father. It would be a buffer from George's impromptu visits.

Marni felt that she was gaining Kimberly's confidence to join the deal. "The wing bordering the woods was made for you," Marni assured her. "It was used by guests visiting for great lengths of time. Nobody wanted to leave such great accommodations. It just oozes with charm." Marni squeezed her shoulders together emphasizing her point. "You're going to flip Kimberly. Every room of the triplex has hardwood floors in perfect condition. There are old wood beams, hand carved wood mantles, and brass fixtures also. Your daughter will come out of this with an incredible teenage haven," Marni suggested. "The third floor is large enough for a bedroom and sitting room." Kimberly moved closer to the railing of the bridge. She stared at the right wing and then studied the rendering that she held in her hand. Marni knew that her bait was working.

Kimberly wandered what she should do. She leaned her elbows on the wood railing. The estate was beautiful. It would be a special home for Candy. She went through a lot in her young life. "What about me?" Kimberly silently asked. It had everything to make her life wonderful. Didn't she need a reward for surviving?

"Where's your place?" Nina asked Marni breaking the silence. "I was going to combine the second and third floors of the mansion and have Kimberly design an apartment for myself and my two sons. What do you think, Kimberly?" Marni didn't anticipate Kimberly's immediate response. "Absolutely. Just tell me what you want," she said turning around. Marni smelled success at her fingertips. A giant step had been taken toward her goal.

"What's happening with the first floor of the mansion? Nina asked.

"I spelled it out in the proposal," Marni said but she gladly repeated it. "Another area for all of us to own and use. When there were no more questions, Marni suggested they move on. But not before she let the women take one more glimpse of the estate from the car. Through the rear view mirror Marni saw Kimberly and Nina wearing smiles on their faces. She knew that they were pleased with what they saw and what they heard. The best was yet to come, the tour of the mansion and its grounds. She was wise enough to say nothing while she drove.

Shortly after Marni entered a brick walled courtyard, she stopped the car. Alan Davidson, the owner of Soundview was walking down from the portico. He could have been a model for a magazine. His charcoal black hair was pulled back tightly into a ponytail. His muscular frame of five feet ten inches was dressed stylishly in a white linen shirt, black slacks and Gucci loafers. Marni knew that he was going to gush with charm. He was a smooth operator. "Hi, Alan," she said meeting him midway along the path. When the women joined her she said, "I would like you to meet Kimberly Mathews." Alan grasped Kimberly's extended hand and with a slight bow kissed her fingertips. Marni noticed Kimberly frowned. She immediately turned Alan's attention to Nina. "Alan," Marni began the introduction, "I would like you meet Nina Levin." He turned to face Nina. "You're a great artist," he said. "I'm really impressed by your work." Alan moved close enough to Nina to bring his lips to Nina's fingertips. Afterwards, Nina fluttered her fingers in air. Marni thought Nina was giving a great performance. "Thank you," Nina said. "I'm impressed with your very beautiful home."

Wanting to keep the momentum to close the deal, Marni directed the women to take a leisurely walk around the grounds. She handed them a pocket size map of the property. She waited until they walked beyond the side of the house. Knowing they couldn't hear her, she said to Alan, "I've already told you on the phone these women qualify to purchase your property. Here's an information sheet on each of them and a write-up describing the purchase proposal." She handed him a white envelope. "I've worked with Kimberly and Nina before. I know that we can close this deal."

"That sounds good, Marni," Alan said. "My creditors won't be satisfied with golden promises. They want green cash, babe, cash that they can see and hold."

"I know," said Marni. Bankers always grilled her about the worthiness of clients that she recommended. She was well aware of their concerns for late payments. Red marks didn't look good when the auditors arrived.

"Knowing isn't good enough," said Alan. "Time is running out. Business is slow. I have to consolidate my holdings."

"Calm down. I realize you're in a bind," Marni said sympathetically. Inwardly, she cringed at the word babe. "I'm trying my best to sell your property."

"Babe, maybe this'll help. I'll include the furnishings of the main floor, except the artworks. I'm sure Nina can put the wall space to good use. I'll even lower the price $100,000. The transaction must be completed within three months."

"Let me think about it for a moment," Marni said with a

smile. She wanted to make the deal but his continued use of 'babe' rubbed her the wrong way. In her plan the first floor would be owned and used by everyone. This would be a great selling point to the women. Everyone liked to hear the owner dropped the price.

"How does it sound?" Alan asked.

"Great," Marni replied. "It would fit in nicely with my proposal." Mentally, Marni had already figured out the new cost of everyone's share.

"I knew you would like it."

"It still doesn't change the short time to take care of everything," Marni said. "The new law relaxes zoning requirements and streamlines the process for rezoning. Three months isn't enough time to close. I need approvals from the Planning Board, the Building Department and the Health Department. Bureaucrats move so slowly and paper you to death. Before any submission, I must get architectural plans drawn up and that'll take time. On the positive side, the women are locked into moving dates. You can help yourself. Allow the renovation to begin when there's a signed building permit and a written mortgage approval. You're exposed to some risk but it would move everything forward. This could be an inducement to have the women close quicker."

"I've no problem with that," Alan replied.

Marni was glad to hear that. She wanted to lock everyone into a commitment to the project. "I'll do my best to meet your time schedule," Marni promised. "After today, I hope to give you a signed purchase agreement and within six weeks a mortgage approval. Your lawyer can probably negotiate some extra time to pay off the creditors with a signed commitment to purchase the property. Think about the up side; your home has just become a viable piece of real estate. Its sale will make you solvent again. You're a very lucky man."

Alan smiled. "It's a pity I'm forced to sell. The property is worth a lot more with the new zoning. If I could wait, I'm sure some developer would give me big bucks for this place."

"In your circumstance there's only one course of action. Accept the purchase offer before you. Be thankful for it. Now I better go find Kimberly and Nina." She didn't want to hang around with him and listen to his bullshit why he shouldn't sell his home. She wanted the property.

Marni found Kimberly and Nina standing silently in awe of the view from the rear patio. The giant maples bordered a freshly mowed lawn that swept down to an in ground pool. Beyond that, white sailing craft dotted the waters of Long Island Sound, sparkling in the bright sun. Off to the right, a stone path led to a well-groomed grass tennis court, and at the end of the walk hidden by tall trees was the brick guest-house.

"Ladies," Alan said approaching the group, "allow me to give you the grand tour."

"From what we've seen," Nina commented turning to face Alan, "I've an idea that we won't be disappointed."

"I'm sure you won't." Alan led the group to the front of the mansion.

"Before we go inside," Marni said, "Alan has sweetened the deal. He has decided to leave all the furnishings on the first floor, except the artwork and has lowered the price by $100,000." Marni knew the women liked the news by their instant smiles.

Nina and Kimberly were the first to enter a two-story foyer with a massive circular staircase outlining the importance of the reception space. "This is something else," Nina declared glancing around. She was already looking forward to her new studio and perhaps her new prey, Alan Davidson.

"Do you like it, Nina?" Alan asked. "And how!" Nina exclaimed.

"I can't wait to show you the studio," Alan replied. "It was made for you."

"What about you?" Nina asked. She wanted a new playmate.

"How much do you pay your models?" Alan asked.

"It depends," Nina said. She wasn't thinking of a financial arrangement.

"Nina, let's stick to business," Marni reprimanded sweetly.

"My god," Kimberly said softly.

"I'm sorry Kimberly," Nina said. "My statement was inappropriate. There's much money at stake."

"I wasn't commenting on what you said but the surroundings." Kimberly had worked on mansions before but this one could be hers. Why couldn't she take a leap forward in her life? Why not become Marni's partner? It could be a testament to normalcy in her life. Kimberly knew that her therapist would support her decision to join the partnership. It would be a commitment to change her prospect for the future.

"Isn't this something else?" Marni asked. She needed to coax Kimberly a little more for her commitment. "Alan, start with the living room," Marni suggested. She was the first to follow Alan through an archway and as always she was immediately captured by the room's elegance. The living room was a study in white—white marble floor, white baby grand piano, and white textured walls. A creamy white modular was the seating in the room. Accessories used to complete the room were in chrome, glass and mirror. The only play of color came from the three large Agam wall panels, the illusions inserted just the right color needed in a monochromatic room. Marni was sure Nina's bold colored abstract paintings would have the same effect. "Smashing, huh," Marni said to Kimberly.

"Right out of Architectural Digest," Kimberly said walking around. She couldn't turn down this opportunity. Soundview will be her new home. The move will initiate the beginning of a new life-style for her and Candy. After hearing Kimberly's reply, Marni knew she had successfully completed the first part of her Master Plan. She had all the players.

"Alan, did you ever sit on these sofas?" Marni asked. She lightly brushed her fingers over the upholstery. "Once," Alan replied jokingly.

Marni laughed. The sofas were in perfect condition. For a second she thought that it would be wonderful if life was so perfect. If it was, she wouldn't be standing there now. "The library is next, Alan," Marni directed.

ON SIX BEAUTIFUL ACRES OVERLOOKING LONG ISLAND SOUND. POOL, TENNIS COURT AND A BOAT SLIP. ALL AMENITIES. SHOWN BY MS. MARNI TAYLOR. INFORMATION UPON REQUEST. CALL FOR AN APPOINTMENT (226) 684-6886.

Chapter One

On Sunday afternoon. Marni arranged for Kimberly and Nina to meet her in the walnut panelled library to workout the management of the estate. To celebrate the move to Soundview, Marni brought with her cheese, crackers and a few bottles of Chablis. She along with the others was lounging on the billowy gray down-filled sofas enjoying the cozy ambience enhanced by a roaring fire crackling in the fireplace. Marni noticed the block of cheese was disappearing. She was glad that she had another one in the refrigerator.

"Mmmmm," Nina moaned, "this tastes so good." She had swallowed a wheat cracker spread with pistachio cream cheese. "I don't care how much cholesterol or fat grams I just ate."

"Chablis is perfect with the snack," Marni said.

Nina sipped from her goblet and smiled. "I better not get hooked on this. I'll be too drunk to paint. But I like your powwows Marni. Are you going to bring treats every time?"

"If you like," she answered. "I'm grateful it all worked out. I was having serious doubts that the legal paperwork and renovations weren't going to be completed before we had to move in. Thank heaven for Paul. The reasnon he's my attorney is because he knows his stuff."

"I'll drink to that. Here's to Paul Silver." Nina lifted her goblet. She was immediately joined by Marni and Kimberly.

"Well let's get started with our meeting," Marni said positioning herself in front of the fireplace.

"A quick one," Nina said pointing her finger.

"I'll do my best. There's lots of stuff to cover," Marni said resting some papers on the marble mantle. She knocked on the mantle twice. "I call the first Soundview Management Board Meeting to order."

"Cut the shit," Nina yelled.

"All right," Marni said sheepishly noticing the two women settled back against the cushions of the sofa. She placed two folders on the coffee table. "Your set of bylaws. Read them at your leisure before the next meeting. Any part can be changed. Right now pull out the paper listing board positions with a description of responsibility." Marni gave the two women time to review them. After a few moments she spoke again. "We already made up a schedule for Bonita and a list of her duties. Alex knows what is expected of him regarding the general maintenance of the property. Bonita will coordinate the heavy cleaning duties with him." Marni saw a sly grin appear on Nina's face. "Alex was a big help," Nina said. "He made my move easier." Marni was bothered by Nina's comment since she had an agenda to accomplish. Nina had other things on her mind. "Do I hear any volunteers for a particular position?" Marni asked. Nina responded immediately. "I volunteer for the outdoor maintenance; that is, if everyone is agreeable." Marni should have known that was coming. "I'll supervise the upkeep of the common rooms," Kimberly said. "I hope, that's also agreeable to everyone." Marni knew that there was only one thing left. "I guess, that leaves me the bookkeeping," Marni said. "Let's keep it simple. We'll have one checking account to deposit the maintenance contributions and its disbursements. We'll have three signatures on the account. There'll be a deposit of $5,000 by each of us, as Paul suggested. The check book will be kept in a common area for everyone to have access. This way, all normal expenses can be satisfied immediately. Just note the balance before writing a check. If in doubt, please use your own check and you'll be reimbursed. If it's a large repair bill, we'll discuss it first. Are we in agreement?" Marni heard both women say, "Yes." Then she continued. "Once a month we'll have a meeting for reporting on our area of responsibility," Marni proclaimed. "I think we should set a definite meeting time. We'll meet the second Sunday of each month except a holiday. Then it goes to the following Sunday."

"Fine," the two women said in unison.

"We'll rotate leadership of the meeting," Marni suggested not wanting to show she had assumed that position.

"You do it," Nina declared. "You're into it."

"I've no objection," Kimberly said.

"All right," Marni replied. "I accept your votes of confidence. I'll do my best to make these meetings short and to the point. Does anyone have business to discuss? She heard two negative replies. "I guess this meeting is over," Marni declared. "The rest of the day is for relaxation." Marni retrieved her wine goblet from the table. "Hooray!" Nina cheered. "I thought of one more thing," Marni quickly added still standing near the table. "I wanted to thank Kimberly for her hard work and the well-designed renovations."

"The thanks should go to the contractors," Kimberly said. "There were also no delivery delays. It was a smooth operation. It was helpful that Alan let us do some prep work once the mortgage was approved."

"You're much too modest," Marni said. "My kids even think you're great. That's a tough approval to get. They're thrilled with their new bedrooms. Patience must be your middle name."

"Thanks, Marni," Kimberly said. "They were fun to do, a relief in a busy schedule. Your sons take after you. Greg and Neil knew exactly how they wanted their rooms. Just like you knew exactly how you wanted the renovation of the two floors. I can say without a doubt the Taylor clan was a perfect client."

"Well isn't that good to hear," Marni said.

"I think you and the kids just won some kind of medal," Nina declared saluting Marni with her goblet. "We'll see if you also get a medal for good neighbor. That decision is still open. Although I must say so far, the living arrangement is working out. After signing the mortgage commitment, I grew very apprehensive. I imagined a giant Noah's ark, with three women, three children, four gerbils, two cats, one colorful parakeet, and a staff of two to maintain this menagerie. There was a chance that we would rewrite the movie script It's a Mad, Mad World but we haven't."

"A toast to Bonita," Marni said. "Without her staying on as a housekeeper after Alan moved, this house might have been a mad world."

The women lifted their goblets again.

"And to Alex," Nina said, "beautiful, muscled Alex. It's a joy to watch him work around the grounds."

"Now it's your responsibility to keep a closer eye on him," Marni said. "I'm sure you're going to hate that."

Kimberly frowned at both comments.

The doorbell rang. Bonita came into the room, followed closely by Don Taylor, his outstretched hand was holding a pair of sneakers. "Just thought I'd drop these off for Neil," Don said to Marni. He greeted the others with a nod. "He may need them tomorrow."

Marni got up from the sofa. "You've already met everyone this past week," she said. She grabbed the sneakers out of Don's hand and dropped them next to the couch. "If you keep stopping by, I'm going to ask you to pay rent. What has it been? A dozen times? We've been living here seven days. Neil has another pair of sneakers." Don's conduct was an embarrassment for Marni in front of others. She wandered what Kimberly and Nina thought of him. "Oh," Don replied, "I thought they were for gym."

"I wish you were as concerned in other areas of the children's welfare." Why did she start? It only brought on his whining act. Marni silently mimicked each word a second before Don said it. "What do you mean, Marni?" Don said. Her Paul Newman look-alike husband was gone forever and in his place was this middle age sad sack. "I'm a good father." Yeah, yeah, she thought. "Why do you always attack me?" he asked. Before Marni could answer him, she saw her younger son walk into the library.

"Hi, Dad," Neil said. "I saw your car outside. What are you doing here?" Don pointed to the sneakers. "I just came by to drop them off," he answered. "How about some racquetball?" Don asked sliding his arm across his son's shoulders. "Go ask your brother to join us." Before Marni could say anything, Neil ran out of the room.

"Don," Marni began, "if you want to take the boys someplace, don't you think that you should discuss it with me first. You're so damn impulsive. Marni stared at Don with disgust.

"What did I do now?" he asked. "Your invitation could've led to a big problem." She didn't want to hear another word from him. However she knew that she was in for it until he left with the boys. "Marni, stop exaggerating. I wanted to play ball with my sons. That's all." It was always what he wanted, Marni thought. He never considered anyone else. "What if the children had to study? They would much rather play ball with you. If I didn't allow them to go with you, then I'm the mean mother. You probably want them to see me in that role. Don't you?" Marni hated this exchange in front of the others. Kimberly and Nina looked like they were spectators at a tennis match. "You're ridiculous," Don said. "I'm their father and I just wanted to be with them." Exasperated, Marni answered, "The children live with me. I know their daily routines and obligations. Speak to me first so that we can arrange an appropriate schedule." How many times would she have to say this? She couldn't wait to have everything written down in an agreement. "I'll do the best I can, but I like stopping by. It seems absurd that I need an appointment to see my own children." She understood what he was saying. In the past he walked into the house and asked his sons if they wanted to play ball. The kid who was home became his playmate. Now it everything changed. "That's a consequence of divorce," Marni declared. She decided to set up rules avoiding this kind of conflict. Marni wouldn't wait for a legal agreement. "I have good intentions," Don crooned with a sheepish smile plastered on his face. Marni shook her head. "I'm not denying that, Don, but they need structuring." She knew that he was just as embarrassed as she was airing their laundry in front of others.

"Ready, Dad?" Greg asked as he and Neil raced into the room. "Let's go."

"I'll have the boys back at five, Marni." Don looked across the room. "Ladies," he said, raising his hand to his forehead.

"Now boys don't forget we're having dinner at six," Marni called after them as her sons neared the front door.

"We won't," Greg shouted back.

Marni rubbed the nape of her neck. "I swear, I feel like Don's mother," she said turning back to the two women.

"He keeps hanging on, doesn't he?" Nina said.

"Even my attorney can't get Don's lawyer to commit to a final agreement. The excuse is Don keeps changing his mind. At least that's what my attorney tells me."

"An attorney can stretch the truth," Nina said. "What makes you think this one is more trustworthy than any other?"

"Paul recommended him," Marni said. "I trust Paul. You could be right though, Nina. Perhaps Steven Butler behaves differently with Paul? Who knows? There's that comradeship between attorneys, the good old boys' club." Marni raised her eyebrows to emphasize her point.

"That's a good point," Kimberly said. "Men have an automatic protection system built into their lives. Information is conveniently suppressed in the back of a locked file cabinet. The excuse is a young man's behavior shouldn't damage his reputation in adulthood. It's amazing how clean a record can be made to look."

Marni didn't want to pry into the meaning of Kimberly's words. Nina got up and walked to the bar. She brought back another chilled bottle of Chablis and filled the glasses.

The short silence was broken by Kimberly's next words. "You know who else protects male spouses," she said. "The courts. They have become the surrogate parents of men." Kimberly sat up straighter and moved to the edge of the sofa. She stared straight ahead. Her voice grew louder. The goblet shook in her hand. "It took a stack of legal papers to have a protection order issued so that George can't come near Candy and myself."

"Oh my god," Nina exclaimed.

"The court isn't sympathetic," Kimberly said lowering her head. "You're the one made to feel guilty."

"Talking about guilt," Marni said, "I had such guilt the first time I went to a divorce lawyer. It was the right move, though. My motherly instincts kept me thinking of the kids. How would they react to their parents separating?" Marni noticed Kimberly wasn't listening to what she said. She was staring at the fire.

"The enforcement of the court order is nonexistent," Kimberly declared softly. "A husband is free to do as he pleases and you and your child are exposed to bodily harm at anytime. Courts and police support George's behavior." She flung her hand in the air spilling some wine on the gray carpet. "Oh, I'm sorry," Kimberly said leaning down to absorb the wine with a napkin.

"It'll be fine, Kim," Nina assured. "It won't stain."

"Lately," Kimberly said sitting on the sofa again, "the newspapers have a few stories of women killed by their estranged husbands. The women had protection orders or tried to obtain one. You wait and see more of these stories will be in the news. Women must do something to change this practice."

"It takes a real tragedy to get something going," Marni said, thinking about how jail sentences finally came about for drunken driving. There were too many unnecessary deaths before the judicial system caught up with social behavior.

"Unfortunately that's true," Nina said.

"Since going to therapy," Kimberly said, "I've learned about various support systems. Perhaps if I knew of them before, I might have left George sooner."

"You don't know that," Marni said. "The world can be a quite cold place."

"You better believe that," Nina added. Wasn't that the reason she moved into Soundview?"

"It's even colder if you're penniless," Marni said, "and have the total responsibility to care for children. I can understand why some women rationalize abusive behavior to a state of acceptance. It's just easier. My divorce attorney told me to consider myself very fortunate. I have the finances and professional position to cushion my divorce."

"Luck has nothing to do with divorce," Kimberly said. "It's a horrible process that has been around for a long time. Dr. Norris, my therapist, says divorce, abuse, and drugs aren't new problems. We just talk more freely about it. Television has influenced this kind of communication." Nina thought that was true. "Sometimes you wonder," Nina said, "if there could be more inspiring stories on television, a success story for every negative one. It might give someone the push to change a lifestyle." Nina was smart enough to realize that wasn't going to happen. Stories of people's success rarely are shown. "You're a success story Kimberly," Marni said. "You did eventually leave George. Think what you've accomplished, a great kid and a flourishing business." "I guess so," Kimberly said. She wasn't ready to tell Marni and Nina the circumstances that provoked her leaving. "I wouldn't want the headlines," Kimberly said. "My daughter doesn't need such publicity, or my business." Marni thought she was right. You needed to believe in yourself to effect change.

"Boredom provoked my divorce," Marni said. "Don and I always had fun together, from making mud pies on the beach to dancing under the stars. Suddenly I woke up and wanted something more. Our conversations were of nothing that mattered. Who cared what team was playing on television? Who cared who was doing god knows what? I wanted to know what he was feeling? He couldn't tell me. Essentially Don stayed the same and still played with mud pies. We've known each other since elementary school. I'm sad we're not going to grow old together but the marriage produced two great sons. You can't beat that." Marni smiled. "I'm happier with myself today. Initially, I accepted that Don and I drifted apart. I became a workaholic. Finding out about the girlfriend, it motivated me to end the marriage."

"That will fuck up a relationship," Nina said. "Didn't you meet some interesting men selling real estate?"

"The kids take up a good deal of my time. I'm too busy putting together deals to think about personal stuff."

"I have some advice for you," Nina said. "It's all right to show your brightness, your business expertise, your dedication, and even your toughness. However you should show the qualities with a splash of sensuality, enough to distinguish you from a man. I think a woman with a penis just doesn't make it."

"Is that your secret for success?" Marni asked.

"I live by that credo." Nina glanced at each woman for a moment. "We're too damn serious," she said shaking her head. "What we need is something to cheer up this group. How about a big bash in celebration of our new homes?"

"Great idea," Marni said.

Nina immediately turned to Kimberly. "What about it, Kim?"

"I still have cartons to unpack."

"We'll have the party in a few weeks," Nina entreated. "Come on. You'll have plenty of time to do everything."

"The move was supposed to be a fresh start," Kimberly said. "You're right, a party will be fun. I'm for it."

"Terrific," Nina said. "I can't wait. It's the beginning of January now. How about having it the end of February?"

"Great," Marni said. "Saturday night."

"Fine," Kimberly said.

"If we divide the responsibility we can pull this off easily," Marni advised. "We'll each have our own guest list."

"I'll make a sketch of Soundview," Nina said, "and have it printed on the invitations. What about some music?"

Marni and Kimberly chorused, "Yes."

"Let me take care of the catering," Marni said. "I'll speak to Victorio of La Trieste. I love his food. I'm sure that he'll even have a suggestion for the music."

"We'll have an eating orgy," Nina said, "and go from there." Kimberly laughed. "Nina," she began, "your enjoyment of life is definitely contagious." Marni reached for a cracker. She was glad the two women were her neighbors. It was foolish of her to think that it didn't matter who lived with her in the mansion.

Chapter Two

Nina standing in front of the blank canvas, watched Alan adjust his position according to her directions. "Perfect," she said picking up her paintbrush, "don't move."

"It's exciting being the first to pose in your new studio," Alan said. "Consider yourself a guinea pig," Nina replied. "I had to do something to get used to the place. I wasn't ready to begin a serious composition." She thought about where she wanted to make her first stroke on the canvas. "That's disheartening," he said. "I thought my nudity was serious material." Nina laughed. "It's useful at times. Now turn to the right," she instructed him. "You moved again. A model must stay still." She watched him for a few seconds. "That's good. Now raise your chin."

"Babe, do you think you could turn up the heat? The useful part of me is turning blue." Nina threw down her brush. Annoyed, he didn't say something before. "Of course," she said. Her tone of voice relayed to Alan that she was pissed. She wanted to get on with the session. "The windows are drafty as hell. You should've replaced them when you owned Soundview." Ah, silence, Nina thought, he knows I'm right. I should let his balls freeze off. "You know," Alan finally said, "I never used this wing except for guests. Any time you can put in a more efficient thermal glass. You bought the view from the windows. That's what sold you, babe." Alan was right. There was something about seeing the water that was good for Nina's psyche. She usually meditated facing the Long Island Sound. "What else will be there for me?" Nina teased.

"You might get lucky later," said Alan. Nina adjusted the thermostat. "Or you," she said. On the way back to her easel Nina pulled up some blinds covering the windows to let in more sunshine. "I like to keep my models happy." He snickered, "I never doubted that, for a moment."

She picked up her brush. "Alan rest your leg on the second rung of the stool," she ordered. "Look toward the wall." She waited until he settled down. With only his lips moving, Alan said, "Nina?" Grateful he kept his pose she immediately responded, "Yes, Alan dear?" She was sorry for her outburst. He wasn't a professional model and she was really only playing at her craft. "I know so little about you," he mumbled. Nina laughed to herself. She wielded her paintbrush and Alan heeded her words. He didn't move. "How can we talk about me?" she asked. "We're always talking about you." Alan's world revolved around satisfying Alan. He was a child in a man's body. "Well now it's your turn," he said quietly. "I'm interested. Tell me about yourself," Alan prodded. "I won't move." Nina was very particular about her models. A fidgety one interrupted her creative process. She aligned her easel and began to paint. She didn't need much coaxing with his promise. "Once upon a time," she began, "are you bored yet?" Nina noticed that he was being a good boy by not moving. "Come on," Alan said.

Nina usually never conversed with the models, preferring silence. It allowed her inner feelings the opportunity to freely flow from her to the canvas. Since this was going to be an addition for her gallery of men she was willing to deviate from the norm. "Here goes, My Life by Nina Levin. It started with a mother who was an art teacher. I'm living the life my mother had been too frightened to pursue. She had always been shy of the label "Bohemian' and never fulfilled her potential."

"You're not afraid of anything," Alan said. "She did a good job not passing on her fears." Nina continued painting, her brush not stopping for a moment. She knew that if she started to think about her mother it would not be the light spirited session that she planned. Finally Nina said, "She was a good mother."

"What about your father? What did he do?"

"He owned the neighborhood candy store. If you wanted the best egg cream in Brooklyn, you went to Pops. He should have written a book describing the characters that hung around the store. Growing up in Brooklyn was quite an experience," Nina said.

"It was probably like growing up in the Bronx."

"I wouldn't know. I've never been to the Bronx."

"Looking at the gallery of portraits, you had no need to go to the Bronx. It looks as if you were kept very busy in Brooklyn. Who are all those men anyway?" Everyone who visited her studio wanted to know about them. "For one thing," Nina said, "none of them are from Brooklyn. They're portraits of men in my life after I left home."

"Why are some of them dressed?" Alan asked. "Didn't you tell me you only painted nudes?" Nina smiled.

"Ah, that's Pierre," she said. She pointed her brush toward the first portrait. A man was dressed in a blue blazer and white slacks with a paisley ascot tucked into a white shirt. He was standing in front of a marble fireplace holding a wine goblet and toasting a painting hung above the mantle. The painting was of a chateau picturesquely set on a green hill surrounded by flowers. Nina stopped working as she spoke and a far away look came into her eyes.

Nina at seventeen years old was sitting on the floor of the Louve. She was dressed in a faded blue T-shirt and a pair of jeans torn at the knees. Her thick, wavy hair flopped in her eyes as she bent over a pad to copy a Renoir.

"Mon cheri, you have much talent," a male voice said.

She didn't respond. The stranger repeated the words for several weeks but Nina remained silent and concentrated on her drawing. It took her professor from the Sorbonne who had accompanied the class on a museum jaunt to introduce Nina and stranger. Sitting in her usual spot on the floor, sketching, she listened to the conversation of Professor Dideron and the stranger who were standing behind her. "She is very talented Professor Dideron," the stranger said. "Nina is one of my best students," the Professor replied. "I have great hopes for her. Monsieur Vinot one day you'll have in your collection a painting by Mademoiselle Levin." The stranger answered, "Perhaps." Upon hearing those words Nina muttered to herself, "From your lips to God's ears."

"Excuse me," the professor said. "Did you say something Mademoiselle?"

"No," Nina quickly retorted.

"Nina," Professor Dideron said, "may I introduce to you Monsieur Pierre Vinot, a friend of the arts."

As Nina stood, her sketch pad and pencil slipped out of her hand. Pierre graciously picked them up and placed them in her shoulder pouch. Then in a resonant baritone voice he said, "Pierre Vinot." Bowing, he took Nina's right hand and lightly kissed the back of it. Nina almost fainted. "You're one of those real gentlemen, huh," Nina blurted.

"That's very gracious, merci," Pierre retorted. "Would you do me the honor of having a glass of wine with Professor Dideron and myself?"

Nina looked across at the six-foot tall man wearing a dark blazer and slacks. Broad shoulders filled the double breasted jacket and his tapered waist was accentuated by the fastened gold blazer buttons. Nina got the impression he believed in fitness. His patrician good looks were enhanced by the bluest eyes, a tanned face and perfectly coifed black hair. It was the ascot smartly swathed around his neck and tucked into his shirt that sent Nina spiraling into orbit. Finally she managed to speak. "How about an egg cream," she said. "I could really go for an egg cream."

"What is this egg cream?" Pierre asked.

"Oh," she answered. "I guess I'll settle for a glass of wine. When you're in France, you do as the French. Oui, Monsieur Vinot. I'll go with you and the professor."

"Did you marry him Nina?" Alan asked. Nina was abruptly brought back to the present by Alan's words. "We had a long and beautiful love affair but no marriage."

"No marriage," Alan said. "Why? For a minute there you looked like you left this planet for outer space." Nina sat on the stool in front of the easel. "He was married," she said softly. "Pierre and his wife lived by some arrangement," she said in a much stronger sounding voice, "and divorce was a no, no. A marriage contract fucked up my life." She could still hear the ringing of the phone in the middle of the night. It was Pierre's son Jacques. His voice sounded close enough for her reach out with her hand and cover his mouth, stopping the words that he was saying. She didn't go to the funeral, not after the experience of her mother's death. Nina received a letter from Pierre's wife Michelline not long after Pierre's death. It said that Nina was especially missed at the funeral. Pierre was buried at the chateau. Michelline appreciated the deep feeling Nina had not only for Pierre but the chateau. She forwarded a letter from Pierre in case of death. It reiterated his parting words the day she returned to New York; "Remember my love, you're never alone. I am in your heart forever. Pierre." Nina had an open invitation to visit the chateau, but she never did. She just couldn't.

"Is he still alive?" Alan asked. Nina had difficulty holding her brush steady. "Oh, I don't want to talk about it."

"Just tell me," Alan insisted.

"He died in a plane crash," she said very softly. "He was going skiing and his friend was the pilot. Small plane, bad weather. What can I say?"

"I'm sorry," Alan said.

"So am I," Nina said in a more normal tone of voice. "We had been living apart for quite awhile but it was good to know he was there . . . if I wanted him." She got off the stool and flipped back her hand with the brush. Then she targeted a spot on the canvas and began to paint again.

"How about the rest of the men?" Alan asked.

Nina ignored Alan's inquiry. She painted silently so she could regain her composure.

"Come on Nina," Alan said. "Don't stop now. How about the rest of the men?

"Oh, all right," Nina moaned. "Keith is the next," Nina said. She knew that her wall was the essence of her personal life. Nobody heard her say the words I love you. She could touch a cheek, an arm or lips but there was no touch returned. There was no portrait of a soul mate whose familiar body entwined with her nightly. The wall was full but her life was empty. She merely rambled on to Alan, her words as meaningless as her life apart from her art. "Keith owned the gallery where I had my first showing in the United States. He fell madly in love with my paintings. My affair with him lasted only as long as the show," Nina said. "I still exhibit in his gallery. He introduced me to

Jonathan, the person in the third painting. Jonathan was the first husband and only husband."

Alan moved slightly, improving his view of the work. The man was depicted with an ingratiating smile and a subtle ease to his stance. Nina had painted everything about him in human form except his eyes. They were of a cunning fox. "Alan, your position is changing again, that's better," Nina said seeing he was just as she wanted him. "Jonathan and I are divorced for many years, but he's still my agent. We now have a relationship that's perfect for both our egos."

Nina noticed an incredulous expression on Alan's face. "Weren't you at all upset when your marriage broke up?" Alan asked. "My divorce almost killed me." That was the farthest thing from her mind. "No. We were very civil about the whole thing," Nina said. There was no deep love there. She married Jonathan on the rebound. She realized leaving Paris wouldn't compel Pierre to divorce his wife. "William, a Texas millionaire is the next painting. He had a sense of humor. It was fun depicting him with a wide rimmed cowboy hat, leather chaps and caressing an oil well. He sent his plane to pick me up in New York and deliver me to his ranch. I stayed with him after the divorce." William was her once biggest collector. She sighed. "He'll always have a special place in my heart." As all her collectors, she thought. It was her only sustaining intimacy in her life.

"What happened to him?" Alan asked.

"He died suddenly one day," she said.

"Nina, is it fatal to have a relationship with you?"

"Look at the wall, Alan. What do you think?"

"I guess I'll take my chances."

"Don't worry, Alan, your life is safe in my hands. When I returned from Texas, I needed soothing. My brownstone in Greenwich Village, a gift from Pierre was destroyed in a fire. As fate would have it, I met Sasha, the next person on the wall. He turned me on to yoga. Our relationship was definitely uplifting, spiritual for me and physical for him." Nina put down her brush and poured a cup of coffee.

"Time for a five-minute break," she said.

"You fascinate me, Nina," Alan said, putting on his robe and taking his coffee. He walked over to a painting of a young man with a white shawl draped around his shoulders. "Tell me who is this?"

"That," she answered, "was my dynamic young rabbi. Making love to him was an incredibly religious experience." They laughed.

Alan wandered over to a painting that exhibited an amazing well-proportioned male body. Nina had captured the man's inner vibrancy. His burnished ebony skin gleamed with the sweat of life. Her eyes lit up. "That was one of my fantasies come true. It wasn't disappointing, I can assure you. I met him at a civil rights walkathon."

Alan walked quickly on, stopping at the next picture. Holding his thumb out, Alan assumed the artist's analytic pose. "Obviously, this must have been your tennis pro. The painting looks incomplete." Nina stepped up beside Alan. She said, "Dick was so conceited that I lost interest, so he didn't need any detail. The same is true of the next two. My accountant is on the left. One good thing did come from our liaison. I became incorporated. The other portrait was of my gynecologist, who thought he was God's gift to women." She was speaking of a man depicted with an undersized penis. "Nina," Alan said, "was he really this small?" Lightly, she punched Alan's shoulder. "It's all in the eye of the beholder," she quipped.

"Time to start working again." Walking back to her easel, she instructed Alan how she wanted him to pose. She watched him rest his arm on his knee and face the wall again. "Perfect," she said. "God, that's sexy." Alan smiled.

Alan not moving his head, used only his eyes to look at the last two portraits. One was of a very muscular man, perhaps a body builder. Nina finished her narration. "Mr. America is my personal trainer," Nina bragged. "He keeps me in shape. Guess what he does for extra money?" she asked.

"He hands out towels in a woman's health spa," Alan guessed.

"You're close," she answered. "Sal is a male stripper. The women love putting dollar bills in his g-string as he gyrates past their tables." She thought including herself.

Nina moved on to the last picture on the wall. Her voice sobered. "I've mentioned Marty to you," she said. "Your young lover," Alan said. "More than that. My protege." She had painted Marty in the same impressionistic style that she had used to paint Pierre, employing a softness of color that reflected her gentle caring for him. Blue water ran off the canvas. A baseball cap trapped between water and sand, waiting for the tide or a young, good-looking man jogging toward it. He was dressed in beach attire, latex shorts outlining his manhood and a white t-shirt plastered to his muscular chest, the spirit of youth bursting through the imagery. "I'm very proud of him," she said. Only the other day, she finally received a letter from him. He missed her and was working long hours but his work was being appreciated by his teacher.

"You forgot one. The man's half-dressed."

"Oh him, he's a politician. You never know his position."

"The collection is incredible," Alan said. He moved from his position to study the portraits again. "I would title it The Art of Stroking by Nina Levin." Examining them again, he said, "Some of them look very real and some look like a composite of people. The works show a variety of technique and thought. I like them. Quite skillful. I'm not so sure they were all intimate interludes in your life."

"Is that the art collector speaking?" Nina laughed. She put down her brush and began taking off her smock. "That's it for today, Alan. Your theory could very well be right, but I'll never tell. The paintings have always stimulated interesting commentary."

He walked over to the easel and stared at his image on the canvas. "Why did you paint me that way?" he asked.

"That's how I imagine you in my mind all the time," she answered. She took his soft member in her hand, and began massaging it, feeling it grow hard and erect, making her painted strokes now reality.

"Baby," he said, taking her into his arms and nuzzling her neck, "your stroking is the best."

"I know," she said.

He placed his hands beneath her sweater and slipped it over

her head. Her sumptuous breasts burst forth into freedom. Fervently, Alan kissed every inch of exposed skin, burrowing his head between her breasts and inhaling their fragrance. Her juices wet the crotch of her panties. He placed her left nipple into his mouth, tasting it gingerly at first, teasing it with his tongue until every nerve in Nina's body was electrified. He abruptly changed to the other breast and sucked it greedily satisfying her hungry desire.

Nina pulled Alan's head away and led him to the cushioned mats on the floor. She stepped out of her skirt and lace panties, every motion graceful and seductive. After laying down, she spread her legs apart exposing her private recesses to Alan's gaze. She tempted him with tantalizing slow erotic movements of her hips. He knelt beside her, kissing her inner thigh. Her skin quivered at his touch. With his fingers he explored her until he clasped her sensitive spot. Slowly he rubbed her very core. Nina purred softly. His stimulation became more intensive as he used his other hand to spread open the outer folds of her womanhood. Nina's purrs became shrieks of ecstasy. Alan replaced his fingers with his tongue. Nina lifted her body off the mat knowing what would happen next. The rapid flicking of Alan's tongue stoked her hot smoldering bit of flesh.

"Don't stop, Alan," Nina commanded, "don't stop." Her muscles tensed, her pelvis rose, and she was lost in the throes of her orgasm. "Now, Alan" she shouted. "Now." It took Alan only a moment to retrieve a condom from his robe and then quickly place it on his hardness. He thrust himself deep within her, and the remaining contractions of her orgasm engulfed his swollen manhood. His sounds of passion reached their peak, as he came intensely, explosively. "That wasn't bad, Alan," she said as her body relaxed with satisfaction. "That wasn't bad at all." Alan kissed her lightly on her cheek. "Thanks for the critique, babe," he said. She glanced at the menagerie hanging on the wall.

Chapter Three

Marni entered the first floor dining room holding a crystal vase of white and pink carnations. She studied the black lacquered table surrounded by twelve Chippendale chairs with silk-covered seats. It was a formal setting. She thought that she was going to a black tie dinner party instead of an intimate gathering with kids and friends. Through Marni's perseverance, Kimberly, Candy, Nina, Greg and Neil agreed to have dinner together. After she placed the vase in the center of the table, she moved six chairs near the walls. The new placement looked good since the walls were covered in tufted egg shell silk to match the cushioned chairs. However, she still wasn't satisfied with the seating around the table. The three chairs on either side of the table looked crowded. She spaced the chairs farther apart but still conducive for conversation. Something, she liked having with her kids. Marni noticed Bonita had already placed on the buffet a tray filled with an ice bucket, bottles of soda, and pitches of water, juice and milk. She shook her head. The black lacquered server was much too fancy for the soft drinks. "Champagne should be there," she said to herself. There's no comfy feeling here. The best feature of the dining room was the French doors. She swung them open. The cold air felt refreshing.

"Hey what are you doing?" Neil shouted running into the room. "It's cold." Marni shrugged. "Oh, I'll close it," she replied. "Where do I sit?" Neil asked. "You, Greg and I will sit here," Marni said pointing to one side of the table. "Kimberly, Candy and Nina will sit across from us. How's that?" she asked sitting down. She left an empty chair on either side of her. "It doesn't matter to me," Neil said slipping into the seat next to his mother. Neil was eleven with a round cherub face and lots of light brown curly hair. "Greg will be right down. He's getting out of his soccer uniform."

Marni heard the front door being closed. "Neil and I are in the dining room," she said serving salad to herself and Neil.

"We're coming." Nina said. "Just hanging up our coats."

Within minutes the six were all seated. Marni filled two more glass bowls with salad and passed them across the table to Kimberly, and Kimberly's daughter Candy. They looked like twins, long blond hair, green eyes with peaches and cream skin. The resemblance was amazing. Marni filled Nina's bowl with salad. "Nina," Marni said handing her a salad bowl filled with greens. "Thanks," Nina replied taking the dish. "You gave me too much." Marni shrugged her shoulders. "So eat as much as you want," Marni said. "We give doggie bags."

The last to receive salad was Greg, Marni's older son. He was thirteen. His olive skin, dark brown eyes and dark hair showed a strong resemblance to his mother, except was taller. "Thanks, Mom," Greg said. "I'm starving." Marni placed the large wooden bowl still filled with salad in front of Greg. "There's plenty more if you want a refill," she said. When it came to her sons, Marni never had a problem with their eating habits. They enjoyed good food and it helped them to maintain a good diet for themselves. Of course, they had their share of junk foods too, but she didn't mind.

"Mom, are you and Dad going to have joint custody?" Neil asked. Afterwards her son stuffed his mouth with a forkful of salad greens.

"Well . . . I wasn't planning on it," Marni answered. "So far your father hasn't requested it. Honey, a piece of paper doesn't make a parent; either he is one or he isn't. Why do you ask?"

"A kid in my class whose parents are also getting divorced asked me. That's all."

"Sometimes parents don't do a good job even if they're not divorced," Kimberly said. "You're lucky if you have loving parents." Her last words brought on memories of a painful time in her life.

Kimberly's father was standing alongside her, watching the neighbor's dogs playing, but not like they usually did—running, jumping, barking at the passing cars. Today they were playing close to each other. Teddy was on top of Samantha, holding her with his front paws, and standing on his rear paws, leaning against her from behind. "What are they doing Father?" Kimberly asked with the innocence of a child eight years old.

Reverend Crowley grabbed her arms and dragged her up the stairs like a rag doll. All the while, he was shouting, "Wantonness is the work of the devil."

They entered the small spartanly furnished back bedroom used for visiting ministers and for scolding. He kicked the door shut behind them. Bringing his face close to Kimberly he said sternly, "Take off your clothes."

"Why Daddy?" she said. In the past he would scold her and slap her bare bottom. "Why? What did I do?"

"Don't ask questions. Just do it, quickly."

She flushed with shame as she undressed, exposing breasts not yet showing a glimmer of puberty. A prickling of fear pierced her young body as she saw her father's staring eyes. "Please don't hurt me," she said, putting her arms across her torso and pressing her legs together. "I'm a good girl."

He patted her flaxen hair, then touched her white arms.

"Please let me go," she begged.

Forcing her arms apart, he pinched each nipple between his thumb and forefinger, bruising the delicate skin.

"No more," she cried out. "No more."

"This is what will happen to you every time you sin," he said. Then he opened the closet door and pushed her to the back dark corner. "Stay in here until this lesson is etched in your brain, and you're worthy to ask my forgiveness." He locked the door.

"Please, Daddy," Kimberly yelled. Her father did not open the door. She only heard him call to her mother. A door slammed, then there were only muffled voices.

"Daddy, please open the door," she begged while banging her clinched fists against the door. "Let me out. Please."

At last she heard someone coming. She rubbed her knees, then moved away from the door. Her eyes blinked with the rush of light.

"Well, Kimberly," Reverend Crowley said, "are you ready to be forgiven?"

Kimberly crept out of the closet. She raised her teary green eyes. "Yes Daddy," she answered, "but I. . . . "

He interrupted her. "Do you ask my forgiveness?"

"Yes Daddy, I do," she said trying to stand up. "But I don't know why."

"You still have not learned," he said. "You don't ask questions about those matters. You just do as I say."

"But, Daddy, I have to . . . " Kimberly was again interrupted before she finished her sentence.

"Silence." He sat on the straight-back wooden chair in the room. "Come here, child," he ordered. He pulled her to him. "Bend over my knees."

She turned away and looked at the bedroom door. "But I . . ."

"Now daughter. Now, or I'll make your punishment twice as severe."

Kimberly leaned her small body over her father's lap, her tender buttocks exposed. Grasping both her wrists in his left hand, her father held her arms behind her back. "This is for your own good," he said. He raised his right arm and slapped her bottom. The white skin became marked by five red welts.

"No," she screamed, "no." Her bladder exploded. The Reverend's eyes bulged with whiteness, and from his crimson forehead spindly veins pulsated blue. The gushing urine saturated his trousers. He beat Kimberly harder and harder. "You will learn," he preached. "Lust is evil and disgusting. You must never defile yourself with it. You must always be pure. My daughter must be pure . . . until you procreate for God. Have you learned now, Kimberly?"

"Yes, Daddy," she whispered. "I have! Please don't hit me anymore." Reverend Crowley made her kneel on the floor. Her knees dipped into the warm puddle. His voice modulated to offer compassion. "As long as you do not sin, you have nothing to fear from me or our God. I forgive you, child," he said. He sprinkled her with her own urine. "Put on your clothes and leave me to my prayers."

"Kimberly," Nina said, "wasn't your father a minister? I bet, he had to give advice all the time." There was no response. "Kim," Nina said softly touching her left arm, "are you all right?" Kimberly felt her foot kicked by Candy. "What were you asking Nina?" Kimberly responded then quickly brought a glass of water to her lips. "I said since your father was a minister, he must have given advice," Nina replied. "That's all. "His words weren't worth hearing," Kimberly said putting down the glass. "Excuse me," she muttered and stood. She left the dining room.

"My mother didn't get along with my grandfather," Candy said. "She told me this when I asked questions about him. He died before I was born."

Marni glanced around the table and noticed everyone was busily eating the dinner that Bonita had prepared and served. Their plates were filled with peppery flavored chicken parts baked until the skin was brown and crisp. The side dishes included brown rice topped with minced mushrooms, green onions and steamed cauliflower. "Bonita the chicken is delicious," Marni said.

"Gracious," Bonita said as she refilled the glasses. "It's my favorite meal."

"Say, guys," Marni said, "how's the new semester going?"

"Okay," Greg said. "So far, I still like my teachers."

"That's good, hon. High school teachers really mean business. They're supposed to prepare you for college.

"I know Mom. I've got so much homework tonight and tomorrow is my first math quiz. It's pressure."

"Don't worry, you have the brains. You'll get it all done. The key is to set up a schedule and stick to it. That'll make your life easier. I use one."

"I'll try that, Mom," Greg said. "It doesn't make me feel better. Let me tell you how I would feel better. You do my math. Be a good Mom. You aced algebra. What do you say?"

"You know your grandpa used to do my geometry," Marni said. "I couldn't understand it. Every day I went for help. Unfortunately, once I was the only one in the class with the right answer. Mr. Glen asked me how I solved the problem. I couldn't remember how grandpa did it. If I close my eyes, I'd feel the hotness of my red cheeks when the teacher thanked grandpa for the answer in absentia. I passed the final exam because I memorized all the propositions and theorems. They were worth 80 percent of the test."

"You're telling me that I'm on my own," Greg said. Marni nodded her head. "You've got it," she said, "except consultation." She patted Greg's back. "Sorry Pal."

"Does that go for me also?" Neil asked.

"Not quite," Marni said grasping Neil's shoulder. "You're still young enough for some direction. How to find information, arrange a report, or work out a math problem but that's it."

"Too bad," Neil replied.

"Be glad you're in sixth grade," Greg said. "High school is a killer."

"Eh, no use worrying about it," Neil answered. "It's going to happen anyway."

"That's the spirit," Marni said touching her elbow with Neil's. Her fingers were too busy picking chicken off a bone. "Gee, thanks Mom," Neil said shaking a bone in her face.

"In health class today, we had a lecture on drugs and alcohol abuse," Greg said. "What drugs did they talk about?" Marni asked putting down her chicken to give Greg her full attention.

"Oh, it was mainly pot," Greg answered. "They said if you smoke one joint, the effects will stay in your blood stream for a month. The high can be for thirty whole days. Hey Candy, you're the oldest at the table. Did you ever try it?" Kimberly's face turned white as she sat. Stay calm, she said to herself. Have confidence in Candy. She will say the right thing.

"Yes," Candy said, "it was okay." Kimberly tried to make her lips smile to support Candy's candor. Then she held her breath hoping Candy wouldn't say anything more but that was only hope. "You're not missing anything," Candy continued. "Please pass the milk Greg." She refilled her glass. "By the way," Candy added looking at Greg, "the high only lasts a little while. It's the garbage that coats the lungs which lasts the thirty days." Kimberly thought she should know. She smoked enough but she prayed to herself that Candy really stopped.

"There are some kids in my grade who use it," Greg said. "Boy, are they nuts."

"I don't use it Greg," Candy said. "It was a one time deal. That's it." Kimberly heard the words that made her heart sink. She knew that Candy was lying but Candy's behavior had been good for a long time. Kimberly decided she wouldn't think the worst. Her investment in Soundview was to be a fresh start for both of them.

"Okay," Greg replied. "You were experimenting, right?"

"Right," Candy answered quickly.

"I hope," Marni said, looking at her kids, "that if either of you are in a peer pressure situation, you'll make the right decision. I see Candy has already made one."

The boys stared at each other.

Nina got up to serve the chicken. Walking around the table, she held the chicken platter in one hand and the rice bowl in the other.

"You're a good waitress," Neil said taking a chicken wing.

"My skill comes from working in my father's candy store. Whether it was after school or on weekends, I served everyone in the neighborhood. The neighbors would stop by, share a little gossip and have one of Pops's famous chocolate or vanilla egg creams. Pops had a great sense of humor and understood people pretty well. He could teach you kids a thing or two."

"Bring him on," Neil shouted.

"Oh, boy, another expert to learn from," Greg said.

"You'd like him," Nina retorted. "Trust me. One egg cream and you're hooked. The candy store was neutral turf for the local gangs. Each leader had his own worn, red leather stool at the counter, and the rest of the gang members had their reserved wooden booths in the back. There were never any fights in Pops's place. Thinking about it now, it was a fun time. The empty stools filled with kids at three o'clock. Angelo was always the first to arrive. He would say "hiya Pops" and then sit on his stool third from the end. I can't believe I still remember where he sat. Pops always asked everyone, 'so what's new'? It was Pops's usual customer greeting. Chicken," Nina said placing the platter next to Greg.

"Once the art teacher was absent from school," Nina explained. "The principal couldn't get a substitute. I took over the class. Old Mr. Hardnuts, our friendly principal, checked in every five minutes. I gave the class an assignment to draw a man or a woman. All the classmates drew bare-assed bodies with big boobs." Nina put down the dishes and cupped her hands. Greg, Neil and Candy laughed. "My father laughed also," she said nodding to each kid. "When he laughed everyone heard it in the store. Anyhow let's get back to when I was a teacher. One guy left his paper white. His excuse was he could only think of a naked broad when. . . ." Nina laughed looking around the table realizing what she was about to say. "I'm sorry," she squeaked sheepishly. "I got carried away with my story."

Neil stood up. "Come on, Nina," Neil said. "Tell us more." Nina looked at Marni. Marni shrugged her shoulders. "Finish it. I can't wait for the ending.

"I was voted most popular teacher," Nina said. "The class wanted me as their permanent teacher. The end."

"That was a funny story," Neil said to Nina.

"You're lucky," Greg said. "Your father sounds like a good guy."

"Lucky for that," Nina replied thinking he was the most loving and understanding father a young woman could have. "I was also lucky to have a good memory. It was important to serve on a first come, first serve basis. I didn't need the toughies of the neighborhood to give me a hard time." Nina balanced the almost empty bowl of vegetables on her left forearm, held the chicken platter in her hand and picked up her dinner plate with right hand. "Ta-daaa," she said. "I was really good." Nina put down the dishes to applause. Taking her seat again she said, "I was also really good turning on the boys. My secret to success was wearing the sweaters that I shrunk. They were tight across my boobs. My jeans were another layer of skin. In those days I never even knew what it meant to be subtle. Today, I know the word exists. That's a beginning for respecting myself. Anyhow, I did have a point to my story. Oh, yes, I was a damn good waitress in a fast food joint."

"Is the store still in existence?" Candy asked.

"Yes, it is."

"My father remarried a few years ago because my mother

died. My stepmother or father's wife, whatever you call her, she's a good woman and great for Pops. Her nephew used to be my father's right-hand man. He bought the store when my father retired."

"Thanks for sharing," Marni said.

"It's my life," Nina retorted.

"Hey, Nina," Neil said from across the table, "you're okay."

"You are too Neil."

"What's for dessert?" Candy asked. She knew her mother had made it. "I tried out a new chocolate cake recipe," Kimberly said. "I hope it tastes as good as it looks." Candy rolled her tongue around her lips. "Your cakes are out of sight Mom," Candy said. "Wait until you all taste it."

"Bonita will serve it when the table is cleared," Kimberly said. Everyone grabbed a plate and brought it to the kitchen. When the table was clean, Bonita brought out a cake with thick swirls of chocolate icing and, in its center, one lit candle.

"Why the candle, Bonita," Greg asked.

"For my family," she answered. "You've been here one month."

"That long," Marni said. "It feels like a real home. What a wonderful miracle."

"Yes, it does," Kimberly said, "it really is a miracle." Silently she said, "Another whole month without a sign of George or my father's curse." She crossed her fingers under the table.

"Who gets to blow out the candles?" Neil asked.

"All of us," Marni said.

Chapter Four

Marni looked at the lucite and gold clock on her desk, a gift from one of her satisfied clients. It was nine o'clock. Where does the time go? She had been working for more than an hour. Her rosewood desk was cluttered with papers. For that matter she had papers and folders on the black leather couch and the smoked glass table she used for sales meetings. Her office was a mess but she had no intention of straightening it. In less than an hour she had a meeting with her divorce attorney Steven Butler. It was important that she call Paul.

Paul Silver was Marni's legal counsel for primarily business matters. However the professional relationship went beyond that and it turned into a friendship also. They met at her first closing when she was a new real estate sales person. The closing went smoothly. She and Paul had kept in touch, drifting in and out of each other's lives. Paul referred clients to her, and she did likewise. When she opened her own business ten years ago, she considered no one else to handle her legal matters. She trusted him.

Marni considered Paul more than just a lawyer but a good friend. She helped see him through a deeply scarring tragedy. His wife, who had been his college sweetheart, law partner and best friend, was run down by a drunken driver. Since that day seven years ago, Paul spent most of his time building up their law practice. To ease his personal loss he became an advocate for imprisonment for drunken drivers. Marni was a board member and coordinated fund-raising events. He also founded a support group for families similarly victimized.

She always tried to introduce Paul to single women she met through real estate transactions or during professional seminars. He would be a perfect date; charming, witty, and intelligent but he never called the women. He showed no interest in a serious relationship.

Paul's secretary answered the phone, recognized Marni's voice, and connected her immediately to his office.

"Hi, Marni," Paul said. "I accept. Name the time and place."

"What are you talking about, Paul?"

"I thought you were asking me out?"

"You must be joking, "Marni replied. "After all this time you want to screw up our relationship? We go back too long for that."

They laughed. Marni pictured his boyish grin, chiseled features, and wavy brown hair easing down his forehead. "Be serious, please. I want some last minute advice."

"Just remember, Marni, I'm always available for you."

"Thanks, Paul. Please listen. I'm going to see Steven Butler in a little while. Any last minute suggestions?"

"You have the list of terms and property that you want included in the divorce agreement.

"Yes. Right in front of me."

"Think of the equity division as a business deal. It's only things. In the end it means nothing. I'm sure Don won't give you a hard time on this. The problem is child support. Stress how you feel. Remember Marni, be calm. Then let Steven go to bat for you and the kids."

"I feel better talking to you."

"I'm sorry I teased you before. I thought, you were reminding me about the party tomorrow night."

"You're coming aren't you?"

"Yes, I am. I'm looking forward to it."

"Thanks for the advice. I better go so I'm not late."

"If you need anything, pick up the phone. Don't forget."

"I'll remember. See you." Again Marni was seated in Steven Butler's waiting room. She looked around the reception room, stopping at the glass enclosure. The secretary smiled. Marni appreciated the gesture.

She glanced at her watch, Steven Butler arrived in the waiting room ten minutes late for the scheduled appointment. His sleeves of his white shirt were rolled up, giving Marni the feeling that he was in his office for a few hours. His thing was to wear a matching tie and suspenders. Every time Marni came to the office his five foot ten inch frame was adorned with a different set. Today the design was a gray paisley to match his charcoal gray pleated pants. His bony cheeks seemed to protrude even more this morning as he leaned over to grasp her hand in greeting. "How is the beautiful princess today?" he asked.

Marni tensed. She couldn't stand it when he called her that, but she bided her time. Smiling sweetly she said, "Fine, thank you, Steven." He escorted her to his office. Once inside he pointed to a chair next to his desk. "Have a seat," he said. Seated, her knees formed a perfect resting place to balance the list. With her right hand she deftly smoothed her hair behind each ears, making sure she was ready for Steven's words.

"I was in touch with your husband's lawyer," Steven began. "Don has agreed to divide your personal property equally. It includes the proceeds from the sale of the house, any savings, and all investments that you own jointly. He would like both of you to sign an adjoining codicil agreement relinquishing any claim to the other's business. You can continue to lease the Seville from his company, if you want."

"That sounds fair," Marni said. "I can't think of too many investments that Don made in his own name. Then again, I didn't always know about Barbara, did I. What else did he say?"

"He will let you keep the white El Dorado." She groaned. "He has no choice. That was a birthday gift. Anything else?"

"He offered you minimum support for the children. Financially, he says that he cannot assume equal responsibility. Your husband feels that you can support the children and yourself. He'll contribute what he can to the children's recreational activities and college expenses. No amount was specified. There was an offer to cover the boys under his medical insurance and to have a life insurance policy with them as beneficiaries."

Marni contained her wrath until he stopped reading from his pad. "Are you finished?" Marni asked. "That's it," he said. Without letting a second pass Marni said, "Why should Don be absolved of sharing the child support with me?" Steve took his time to reply. "Be reasonable," the attorney said. "You can afford to take care of them." Marni thought she was being reasonable. Don was the father and should accept responsibility.

"Why should I be the only one to be reasonable?" Marni asked. "Don can afford to take care of them too. Who are you representing here?" She was irritated by the laid back vibrations that she was getting from Steven. Were Kimberly and Nina right? Courts protected the men and lawyers. Was there some secret society where all males take a blood oath? Then she stopped herself from letting her mind run wild with all sorts of ideas. Was she just being paranoid because of her inner turmoil? She looked at Steven. "You're upset, aren't you?" he asked. "Good observation!" Marni exclaimed.

"You're my client, Marni," Steven said. "Please remember that. I'm representing you. I want the children protected too. You can protect them. Judges these days don't automatically award everything to the wife."

"Were you listening, Steven? I'm not talking about myself. I'm referring to my children. I hope you don't want to penalize a woman for being financially successful in business. You're not a chauvinist, are you?"

"My wife died in childbirth. I brought up my daughter alone. I've been breadwinner, mother, and father to her, and we have a wonderful relationship. I did it. Why can't you?"

"What does that have to do with me?" Marni exclaimed. "Your circumstances were different. If your wife was alive, she would have shared the responsibility. Don isn't dead, at least not yet. He shouldn't be treated as if he is. He told the children in my presence how dedicated he was to them and how he'd always be there when they needed him." Marni's cheeks grew red as she hurled her words. "Now he has said this? It makes me furious to see men leaving their homes, excising themselves from their children, leaving the wife to pick up the pieces, while they go off on their merry way, seeking the thrills of the moment. In Don's case it is even more irresponsible. He can well afford to support his children. It won't be a strain on his life-style as other men."

"Settle down. Your anger is making you very stubborn and is getting in the way of your intelligence. Why bother fighting Don? You'll only create a big, ugly scene. Do you want to put your children through that? They would suffer for it. I've seen it happen often. The children become the pawns in an argument while you transfer your resentment of Don to the child support agreement. Don't you see what you're doing? A lot of hate builds up in the breakup of a family. It's difficult to recapture a loving and caring relationship at the end of the divorce process."

She looked at Steven. Some of what he said made sense. Why was she pressing so hard for Don to contribute his equal share? Did she want to punish him, or did she think this would make him grow up? Neither was important. There was a responsibility to the children. "I can appreciate your thoughts but what about children's rights? That's what I'm advocating. It's not for myself. If I don't represent the children, then who will? I will bring the children to this office, if necessary, and they can state, both to you and to Don, what their concerns are. Let them enter a separate agreement with him."

"All right, Marni," Steven said. "I'll research legal agreements made between parent and child. We'll be prepared if the case goes to trial."

"Thank you." Marni took the sheet of paper from her lap and handed it to Steven Butler. "This is a list of terms that I want included in the agreement. We have discussed some of them already. If a question arises concerning any of them, please contact me." Marni stood. "Steven, in the future please refrain from discussing your personal life. You're here to help me and I'm paying dearly for that service."

Marni turned toward the door and Steven followed her out of his office. In the reception room she extended her hand to say good-bye. Steven clasped. "You're one tough individual, my dear," he said. Marni smiled. Since he believed that, she decided to reiterate her position. "Remember I want an agreement that Don shares 50 percent of the financial responsibility regarding the children. Have a good day." She started to walk out of the office but changed her mind. Paul told her to control herself. Holding the door open, she turned to face Steve. "By the way," she said to him, "I think your daughter is lucky to have you as a father." She tilted her head and added, "I think." Steven stood there for a moment. "Women," he said to her.

"Damn feminism." Marni kept her cool. "Only sometimes, Steven," she said. "Don't forget, you have a daughter."

Marni went back to her office satisfied with her meeting. She busied herself with last-minute details for the house-warming party. This was going to be great publicity for her real-estate company. She could hardly wait.

Chapter Five

Marni spotted Paul entering the vestibule and waved. He looked handsome dressed in a dark blue suit. She only had to walk a little way before they greeted each other by exchanging a friendly kiss. "I'm so glad you're here, Paul," Marni said. "You haven't been to one of my parties in a long while. I lost count the number of years." "Tonight was perfect timing," he said. "I couldn't turn down three clients." When Paul called to accept the invitation, Marni told him that his name was the only one to appear on all the guest lists. He had been amused and flattered by the compliment.

"You look ravishing," Paul said clasping her hands. "Red is your color." She removed her hands and curtsied. "You're prejudiced," she said. "You always tell me how great I look. But thanks anyhow, I like to hear it."

Marni quickly glanced around. "Isn't this place fantastic, Paul?" The mansion was buzzing with excitement. "Driving up the road with all the lights turned on," he commented, "the house was quite a sight to see." She knew what he meant. "That's why I bought it," she said slipping her arm through his. She led him into the living room, where they were immediately deluged by a cacophony of music from the five-piece band standing off to one side of the fireplace. Marni scanned the clusters of colorfully dressed guests. Some were dancing, and others were chatting and drinking. Paul took two glasses of pink champagne from a server in a tuxedo. He handed one to Marni.

"I now know why the closing went so smoothly," Paul said, admiring his surroundings, "despite the fact there were so many people involved." Marni had a lot of confidence in herself as an individual. However, every time Paul gave his approval, she felt, her decision was even more perfect. "In the future, I need a complete tour." Hearing Paul's words, Marni was excited. "Would you like to see more right now?" She didn't wait for his reply. She took Paul's hand and steered him toward the staircase.

Marni pressed her code into the pad, and when she heard a click; she turned the brass knob. A few steps brought them into a spacious entryway to a great room combining the living room and dining room. The living area was decorated tastefully in black and white with touches of red. Marni was proud to show it off. Leaning against one black sofa flanking the fireplace, she watched Paul slowly tour the living room.

"What's this?" Paul asked lifting a white object off the coffee table. Marni was proud of her trophy. "The jaws of a shark," she said. "I told you about my adventure." Paul inspected what he was holding. "Off the coast of Spain?" he asked. Marni nodded. "Good memory," she said. "Puerto Banus, to be exact," she declared. "You must visit it sometime. The port is between Marbella and Esta Pona on the Costa Del Sol. Some of the grandest yachts flying flags from all over the world are moored to the docks. Don and I have been there several times. I love to sit at one restaurant along the walkway, have some gazpacho and people watch. It's an endless fashion show as the tourists parade by. An English captain has been docking his fishing boat there for the past fifteen years. He dared me to go deep-sea fishing. I can't put in words the excitement of catching that shark."

"I know the feeling," Paul answered. "I've gone deep sea fishing often. It's one of my favorite sports, but I'm sure I'd enjoy it more with you." Paul replaced the jaws where he had found it and walked to where Marni was standing. He lifted her chin. Her eyes met his. Softly he said, "I'd enjoy everything more with you." Marni was caught off guard not only by his statement but by his closeness. She took a step backward. "What are you drinking?" she asked, needing an excuse to leave the room. "I'll have an Absolute, straight up." She went into the kitchen to prepare the drinks. The scent of his after-shave lingered on her body. It stirred emotions that she hadn't felt in years. Was she ready to pursue this?

Marni poured the drinks and brought them into the living room. The voice of Barry Manilow singing "With You I'm

Born Again," greeted her. She handed Paul his glass and joined him on the black leather couch. "To good times," she toasted. She touched her glass with his before they drank. "I like this song," Marni said swaying to the music. "Dance with me," Paul requested taking the glass out of her hand. Before she responded he helped her off the couch. He placed his arm smoothly around her waist and gently drew her to him. He brushed his lips against her hair, against her ear, and then against her cheek. She was mesmerized by his deep blue eyes. Without the need to say a word, she allowed herself to be kissed intimately. She exchanged her passion with his. "I've waited a long time to do that," he whispered into her ear. "A very long time."

"We're friends remember," Marni said meekly, moving away. "This shouldn't be happening." Paul drew her closer again to him. "Let's become kissing friends from now on," Paul answered. "How about it?" His lips met hers again and Marni felt powerless in his arms.

Realizing they could miss the party, she gently pushed him away. "I think we better finish the tour," Marni said. She walked across the great room to the area designated as the dining room with a white marble table. Paul followed her. "Whose idea was to have no walls between the rooms?" Paul asked. "Mine," Marni replied. She liked the fact he seemed to admire the interior design. "It's a fetish of mine, having dinner in front of a burning fire. It sets a mood."

"I hope you were thinking romantic," Paul said embracing Marni again. "Do I get an invitation?" Marni hardly moved her lips when she answered, "What do you think?" She couldn't believe that her hands usually cold were hot and sweaty. Paul kissed her cheek and said, "I think yes."

"Then I guess you have to see the kitchen where I'll cook the meal." She led him around a block glass wall and entered an ultra modern kitchen in finished white wood and stainless steel. Paul looked around. "I expect a real gourmet dinner with this equipment. Don't disappoint me," Paul said tapping lightly Marni's nose. She took his hand and moved him along a hallway. "Let me show you the media room." They walked into a room with tan ultra suede couches matching a Berber carpet. One wall was covered with a forty-six-inch television, a VCR, stereo system with speakers installed around the room. A pinball machine was tucked in the corner. "The family playground," Marni exclaimed."

"You thought of everything," Paul said.

"Kimberly helped me with some decorating. She did a wonderful job," Marni said. "She also designed this staircase to the third floor. Greg and Neil have their own bedroom, bathroom and study. There are two guest rooms. Finally, I have a master bedroom suite that's something else. Wait until you see it. I have a hi-tech unit that has a steam shower and jacuzzi. My bedroom is my favorite room." After Marni said that she felt her face flush. She was still embarrassed a few minutes later when she turned on her bedroom light.

"A king-size bed for just you," Paul said.

"I like to roll around." Marni couldn't believe her words. Why did she say that? The words seemed to come out so naturally expressing some deep dark feeling buried away in the corner of her heart. "I'll remember that," Paul said patting the bed. Would she have him keep his promise? What was happening here?

She followed Paul into the bathroom. Across the back wall was the deluxe unit complete with a tub and shower. "How did they get all this into the bathroom?" She smartly replied, "It comes in parts. I had to have it. I take a steam and jacuzzi every day to calm me down from the stresses of the office." Marni opened the door to show him all the fittings. "Can this be the dessert when you make me dinner?" Paul asked. "I'll put that on the menu." She hesitated in the bathroom doorway before she turned off the light. "Paul let's not rush anything," she said. "Yesterday you were a very good friend. Tonight, I'm feeling something more. But I'm still in the midst of a divorce. Do you understand what I'm trying to say?"

"Yes, completely. Steven said the divorce agreement is almost in place."

"You spoke to him?" Marni was surprised by the revelation.

"Yes. Just looking after your interest."

"I see." She closed the bedroom door and was about to walk

on when Paul grasped her shoulders. "I want it to feel right for the both of us. It'll take time but I'm sure we'll get there." He seemed to know what he wanted. Marni liked that in a man. "Are you Mr. Perfect?" she asked. If she allowed herself to think about it now, she would've had her answer.

Before they returned to the party, he kissed her again, deeply, intensely, imparting a covenant for the future. Marni slowly walked down the stairway with Paul at her side. She let the sounds of people having fun draw her back to the party. Entering the vestibule, Marni and Paul were immediately joined by Nina and Alan.

"You girls did a wonderful job organizing this bash," Alan said to Marni.

"Stop calling us girls," Marni said. "To be socially acceptable, call us women or ladies but not girls."

"What's the difference?" he said.

"It's the twentieth century," Marni said caustically. "I'm not going to debate this with you."

"You women did a wonderful job organizing this bash," Alan said with a slight bow. "Is that better, Ms. Taylor?"

"Yes, Mr. Davidson, much better. Continue with what you wanted to say."

"Thank you," Alan said. "The food is outrageous. I've already tried the stir-fried veggies and seafood crepes. When I get finished with the buffet tables, I'm not going to eat again for at least a day."

"Thank Marni," Nina replied. "She worked with Victorio of La Trieste."

"And who found those Marcel Marceau rejects?" he asked. Alan pointed with his hand toward the mimes mingling among the guests. They were performing ordinary actions like opening a door, peeling an apple, and stepping over a puddle of water. "I must admit, I do find them amusing."

"What's bugging you, Alan?" Nina asked. "You're sounding more obnoxious tonight than usual." She gave his shoulder a shove. "Don't come down on me like your friend here," Alan said to Nina. "There's something the matter," she said pulling on his sleeve. "What is it?"

"Nothing," Alan said. "Don't be a nag."

"I thought only wives nagged, not lovers," Marni quipped. "I have a lot to learn about the single life."

"Nina, I pay my shrink one hundred and twenty-five dollars an hour for the privilege of listening to me," Alan stated frankly. "Since I have his expert opinion, I don't need yours."

"Oh, my," Marni said, "another man who needs a shrink to hold his hand. What is this world coming to?"

"Stop making fun of me, Marni," Alan said. Then he turned back to Nina. "Come on, Nina. This is a party. We're supposed to have fun. Let's get a drink. You need to unwind."

"You can't fool me," Nina said. "I know you . . . remember? Besides, you can't hide from the observant eye of the artist."

"You better say something Alan," Paul said, "or else you're going no place."

"Okay. Okay. I'm green with envy," Alan said, his eyes followed his hand brushing off an imaginary speck of lint from his black silk shirt. "I miss my house. That's it, nothing more. I've said it, now let's move on."

"You get points for honesty," Paul said. "Right, Nina?"

"There's nothing like honesty between lovers," Nina answered, pressing the point of her finger into Alan's chest. "Now we can see what exotic drinks the bartender can create for us. Come along, lover."

"Marni, Paul, are you coming?" Alan asked.

"No thanks," Marni said. "You go ahead." They headed toward the bar in the living room. Nina looked very elegant in a black knit dress outlining her perfect figure. The turtleneck of the dress was encircled with a unique solid gold neck piece with insets of diamonds and emeralds. Marni thought that Nina's appearance would capture a stare or two.

"Marni do you mind if I say hello to a few people?" Paul asked. "I hate to leave you even for one second."

"That's fine," Marni said. "I'll be moving around. Catch up to me whenever you like." From Marni's vantage point in the foyer, she studied the heterogeneity of the party and decided the three guest lists meshed well. It pleased her to see that everyone was circulating and by the constant chatter, she knew the party was a success. Lulls in conversation meant boring. She noticed her banker standing near the door of the living room and speaking exuberantly with Wayne Whitney, Kimberly's associate. She thought that a deal might be in the making and tucked the idea in the recesses of her mind. Nina and Alan joined a man inspecting the artwork on the living room wall. Marni guessed he was Jonathan Parker. She almost didn't recognize him wearing clothes. Nina kissed him, and the two men shook hands. Marni hoped after all the agreements were signed that she and Don would be as civilized.

Marni headed for the library after she noticed Henry was having a drink with Kimberly. Kimberly looked like a dream in her forest-green suit. Her long blond hair was twisted into a French knot. She matched the elegant appearance of Henry Gordon in a black suit. His full beard neatly trimmed and his muscular body showed that he practiced what he preached, a healthy mind belonged in a healthy body. He also had a fine reputation as a psychiatrist. A momentary pang of regret whisked across Marni's mind. It was too bad Henry couldn't help her have a healthy marriage. Don, she knew, was still using him as his therapist. Don would have loved this party. He was great at small talk. After all, he had kept her amused for sixteen years, or at least twelve of them. She laughed to herself, then walked toward Kimberly and Henry.

"Having a good time?" Marni said. "I think everything is going great," Kimberly said. "I agree," Henry said. "Kimberly has been filling me in on all the renovations that went on." Marni knew Henry for many years. When his wife was alive, the two couples would sometimes go to dinner. Now she just saw him at the hospital and museum board meetings. They were both members. She thought it was a good idea to introduce him to Kimberly. He loved playing tennis with good players.

"Isn't this place incredible?" Marni said. "It is," Henry answered. Marni wasn't getting tired of all the favorable remarks about the mansion. She hoped that she could put together similar investments.

"You're functioning well these days Marni," Henry said. "Is that a statement or a question?" she asked. Marni felt sometimes Henry played the psychiatrist too much. "What would you like it to be?" he replied. "Why do you always answer a question with a question?" Marni retorted. "We're not in session." Henry bowed. "Touche', after all these years it's a habit. Seriously, how are things?"

"Hectic but invigorating. I think Don and I are getting closer to an agreement, at least the part between us. The major obstacle is child support. I want Don to assume half of the monetary obligation for the children." Marni mentioned it hoping Henry would discuss it with Don.

"He should," Henry said. "He's the father and has the resources."

"Maybe you can tell Don that."

"What I discuss with Don is off limits. You know that."

"I'm sorry. I got carried away." If she were a betting person, she would put money on Henry discussing it with Don, anyway. "You're my friend. I don't want you to feel uncomfortable in my presence."

"Thank you for saying that," Henry said.

"Marni," Nina said, "can I see you alone?"

"Excuse me," Marni said. "What's wrong Nina?"

"Don is here. He seems very drunk."

"Oh shit," Marni said. "Not tonight."

She and Nina approached the front foyer. Don was standing there, swaying, a drunken smile plastered on his face. "Hi, Marni," he said.

"Please turn around and leave," Marni said in a low voice.

"Aren't you going to offer your husband a drink so we can toast your new home?" he slurred.

"You've had enough to drink. What are you doing here?" Marni asked, thoroughly annoyed. "Why aren't you with Barbara? Did you two have a lover's quarrel?" Marni stopped berating him when she saw the hurt look on Don's face. She continued gently. "Don, you wanted to live your life. This," she said, gesturing around her, "is mine. Why do you keep coming back?"

"I don't know," he answered. "Henry would probably say this is not appropriate behavior, but here I am anyway."

"Well, since you know you aren't supposed to be here, why don't you leave."

"Come on, Marni . . . just one drink. Have a heart."

Marni was grateful when Henry walked over. "Maybe you can persuade Don to leave," Marni said to Henry. Don grimaced at Marni's words. She thought he was also annoyed that Henry was at the party. "So," Don said, "you've switched sides, Henry." Marni was glad Henry didn't reply instead he requested his coat from the attendant. "I'll call a taxi," Marni said walking away. As the door closed, she heard Don say that he didn't want to leave. He wanted to have a drink with her. Marni felt sorry for him. He looked so pathetic. After she called the taxi she joined Nina and Kimberly in the library.

"Are you all right, Marni?" Kimberly asked, thinking she wasn't alone when it came to spousal problems.

"He looked like a lost puppy dog," Nina said.

"I know," Marni said. "Just give me a minute to compose myself. Don might think I'm always in control, but he knows how to get to me."

Paul appeared with a small tray of four drinks. "I guarantee you instant well-being," he said to Marni handing her a drink. "I mixed them myself."

"It seems," Alan said, as he joined them, "we had a party crasher." Marni stared at him while she used an imaginary laser beam to obliterate him. "Not very funny, Alan," Marni said. "Hopefully, no one noticed." A quick glance around and the upbeat party noise put at rest her concern. "He didn't look like a bad sort of chap," Alan said. Four pairs of eyes glared at him. "Just kidding," he said, "just kidding."

Marni saw Henry enter the library. She immediately went over to him. "How's he doing?" she asked. "He's having the normal problem of cutting the umbilical cord, that's all," Henry answered. Marni couldn't believe what she was hearing. "That's all," she said repeating his words out of total frustration. "He's driving me crazy. Instead of your therapy sessions, perhaps you should give him a pair of scissors. They might be more effective." Marni knew that she wouldn't get a rise out of Henry. He was always in control. He lightly touched her shoulder and said, "I understand how you're feeling, but time is the antidote for many problems. Please be patient." Marni realized Henry was right but it was too damn difficult for her to accept it. There was nothing more to say about the incident right now with a party in progress. "Thanks for your help," she said seeing her friends looking in their direction. "Let's join the others, Henry. You deserve some fun." Once Marni reached Paul, she wasted no time asking him to dance. She had a strong suspicion his arms around her would put her back in a party mood.

Chapter Six

"Buenos Dias, Senora," Bonita said. "Cafe?" Bonita kept the electric coffee pot on the peninsula counter, a kitchen divider between the cooking and eating area. "Si, Bonita," Nina said. "Muchas gracias."

"Hi, Nina," Marni said, "come join us." She and Kimberly, adorned in only the barest of essentials, sweat shirt, warm-up pants and minimum make-up were sitting around the glass-table drinking coffee. "Did you just get up, Nina?"

"I never went to bed . . . correction, I never went to sleep last night," Nina said, sitting. "Alan has his shortcomings, but coming isn't one of them. Kimberly, could you pass the milk, please."

Kimberly admired the natural way Nina went from talking about sex to milk for her coffee. She couldn't even sit through an x-rated movie by herself. "Your presence was definitely missed on the clean-up squad," Kimberly said. "Next time we have a party, you're the captain."

"It was worth it," Nina said. "Do you think everyone enjoyed themselves?"

"Yes, I do," Marni said. "They stayed until three o'clock in the morning. I thought, everything was perfect except the incident with Don. Henry said Don just needs time. I hope he's right. By the way Kim, what do you think about Henry?"

"I enjoyed talking to him," Kimberly answered. "He was very understanding while self-confident. It was easy being with him."

"Has Henry gained a new fan?" Marni asked.

"If he continues to make me feel good about myself," Kimberly replied.

"I know what you mean," Marni said.

"What was Paul doing up in your apartment?" Nina asked Marni.

"I was showing him around."

"That's all?" Nina said. "My intuition tells me otherwise."

"That's all I care to discuss."

"When I came down this morning," Kimberly said, "I scouted out the situation. We have tons and tons of food left over. I'll help Bonita set up some trays in the library. Would you like that?"

"Absolutely," Marni said. "We're scheduled for our monthly meeting today. Don't worry, a short one."

"You better," Nina said.

• • • • •

Nina leaned over a tray of hors d'oeuvres on the coffee table and popped one in her mouth. "The stuffed mushroom is still fabulous. It's even better today than it was last night. Who wants one? Kim? Here, Marni, try one." Nina brought some over to the sofa where Marni had just seated herself and was sipping wine. "Your reward for a short meeting." She left a few on a plate in front of Marni. "You seem to have recovered from last night's episode with Don." Nina took another mushroom before putting down the tray.

"I'm still a little angry," Marni said. "He's such a child."

The doorbell rang. Nina went to answer it. "I wonder how he feels," she called back over her shoulder. "I wonder," Marni echoed. Instinctively, she followed Nina to the door, holding her glass of wine. "Speak of the devil," Nina said swinging open the door. Marni annoyed to see Don so soon again spilled some wine out of her glass onto the floor. "Damn," she said seeing the red splotch on the white marble tile.

"This must be 'our' spot," Don said to Marni. "I seem to remember we were standing here last night."

"I'm surprised you remember anything," she said wiping the wine off the floor with a tissue. "Why are you here?" Her tone was one of exasperation. "The boys weren't supposed to be back yet." With the floor clean, Marni stood up and faced Don.

"I came alone," he said softly. "I wanted to apologize." Marni moved closer to him and spoke just as softly. "Leave," she said gritting her teeth. "Turn around and go."

"Forgive me, Marni. I had a little too much to drink and felt sorry for myself. All I wanted was to see you."

"Why Don?"

"We're still married, you know."

"Only on paper," Marni retorted. "The decision is already made to get a divorce. Now, you have to work it out with Henry or Barbara or both. You have your life. I have mine. Weren't you the one to say, a little pain at the start, for much happiness later? Believe in your bullshit. Do us both that favor." Marni opened the door. Don ignored her gesture and instead whispered in her ear. "Who did you fuck last night?" he said. "Did he know all the right spots?" Marni feeling Don's comment was offensive wouldn't let him get away with it. She replied, "No problem, he was a fast learner." Don grimaced. "I can never win. You're a bitch with all the right answers." Marni was disgusted with Don and just wanted him to leave. "No, Don, I'm merely finishing what you just started."

"I'll bring the boys back later." He turned, made a supreme effort to straighten his shoulders, and walked out the front door.

"I hope the boys didn't see you drunk last night," Marni called out after him, and then slammed the door.

"Damn it," Nina said. "Don wants his nookey on the side while having his good wife at home so she can wipe the kids' tears and the big boy's ass." Marni thought Nina had made a good point. "You definitely have a way with words," she said to Nina returning to the library. "You're not too bad yourself," Nina said refilling the glasses.

Marni swung her goblet in the air. "What the hell," she said and drained the liquid to the last drop. Marni nestled her body into the sofa cushions and sat looking into the fire. She drank the wine to smooth over the raw edge from her encounter with Don and satisfied her appetite with the abundance of food. The soft glowing fireplace partially masked the faces of Kimberly and Nina and created for Marni a safe place free from stress. Her space was suddenly invaded by Nina's remark.

"I'm still wet from last night," Nina boldly stated standing.

She pulled her jeans downward from her inner thighs. "The only thing missing was a mirror above my bed." She sat again and put her head back to look at the ceiling. "I would have definitely enjoyed watching us, but I can't imagine being more turned on."

"It was just a few months ago," Kimberly said, her voice no louder than a whisper, "I was lonely then . . . so very lonely . . . ." Marni and Nina leaned forward, wanting not to miss a word. Kimberly shifted her position on the sofa, her long lithesome body curling catlike on the cushion. "I remember it clearly. There were mirrors on the ceiling but they didn't help. It wasn't the man's fault. He was really quite sweet, an architect that I had known for years. We had ended our evening in an adult motel. He wanted to . . . I . . ." Kimberly paused and closed her eyes. "It wasn't very satisfying. I've never really had an orgasm." She opened her eyes to look at the other women. "There, I've said it and you're not my therapist."

No one spoke for a long time. Marni broke the silence. "Kimberly, I'm glad you felt comfortable with us to share your private thoughts."

"I can't believe what I just revealed." Kimberly's cheeks were flushed, a bright red in color. "Gosh, I surprised myself while feeling relieved. I owe alot to Dr. Norris. She really has helped me." Kimberly emptied her glass of wine. She noticed Marni and Nina remained silent. "I'm sorry," Kimberly said, "I didn't mean to be a show stopper." She laughed. "I guess something has rubbed off since meeting you, Nina. I developed a sense of humor." Nina joked, "That ain't bad. Do you want to go for an encore, Kim?" Kimberly shook her head. "I think I'll pass," she said.

Nina tapped on the table and announced, "Drum roll. Drum roll." She stood and walked in front of the fireplace, assuming center stage. "A few years ago, when I was living in Dallas I had a one woman show. To celebrate the opening, the director of the museum held a bash in the patrons' private dining room. I spent over three hours greeting everyone. After awhile, it grew tiresome. I spotted a man standing alone on the far side of the room. He wore a white cowboy hat perched jauntily on top of his dark brown hair. Did he look sexy, all six-foot-four of him?

His jeans left little to my imagination, and his leather boots with shiny silver spurs certainly stirred mine." Nina's eyes twinkled at the memory. "A fringed shirt, open to his waist, was the backdrop for a badge. Can you believe that? A badge. I caught his eye and gave him the come hither look. Four giant steps brought him with his big, baby blue eyes beside me. He tilted his hat and said, "Hello Mam. Ah laiked yaw paintings and ah bet I'd laik you too. Would y'all laik to join me fol a beer?" Nina put her fingers in her belt loops and stuck out her chest. "Half an hour after we had finished our beers, and bought some condoms, I was riding in the saddle on this wonderful cushy waterbed surrounded by mirrors. He turned out to be a Texas Ranger. Now I know why the saloon gals waited for the rangers to come to town." Nina laughed enjoying Marni's appreciation of the story by her feverish clapping.

"I just can't get over how blase you are about going to bed with a man," Kimberly said.

"I'm casual about it, because of the circumstances," Nina replied. "The way it just happened. It was fun. Everyone should have some fun in their lives. The vagina is like any other part of the body, if you don't use it, it atrophies."

"Hear, hear," Marni said. "I can see how your gallery of men came into being." Marni joined by Kimberly raised their goblets in homage to Nina.

"On behalf of married couples," Marni said, "I would like you to know that they like mirrors also. For our tenth anniversary, Don and I went to the Poconos. You know, to one of those honeymoon havens. A king-sized bed with a mirrored headboard was smack in the center of the room. At the foot of the bed was a heart-shaped tub with mirrors covering every inch of the ceiling. Dark pink flocked paper covered the walls, typical of a bordello, at least, from the pictures I have seen of those establishments. The decor was really a turn-on. We didn't stop screwing that whole weekend." She sat back in her chair and smiled dreamily. "Ah," she reflected, "I miss the sex, not the marriage."

Kimberly, sitting upright against the back of the couch, had listened to each narrative. She had filled and emptied her glass several times. "I wish," Kimberly said, just loud enough to be heard, "I could be as relaxed as both of you about sex." She sat quietly for a few moments, holding her wine glass, her eyes following her finger around the rim. "This is hard for me to talk about." She got up and went for a refill. Kimberly returned to her chair and sat. Lowering her head, she said in a soft voice, "I had a strict upbringing, my father being in the church and all. I had been taught to believe that making love was a wifely obligation to be tolerated, not enjoyed. When I met George and we married, that's all I could do, was just tolerate. I thought, he was satisfied. He told me that he was but since then I've discovered otherwise." She hesitated. "George had been cheating during our marriage. My response was to develop a relationship with another man. It was disaster. The closest I came was to that architect in the motel room. Dr. Norris is trying to help me. I probably should have gone with George for help, but I was embarrassed, and George never suggested it. Most likely, he would have refused if I wanted to go. I started going to therapy after my divorce. I think, now, I could possibly try to have a relationship. At least I would know what makes up a good one. Maybe, this would help me be freer and let myself go with a man like the two of you."

"You're headed in the right direction," Marni said.

"Maybe," Kimberly said, thinking these women, the only real friends she ever had, believed what she said. She couldn't tell them the whole truth. She just couldn't.

"Everyone has problems of one kind or another," Marni assured her.

"They seem to haunt my life," Kimberly said. Lately, she had been feeling her father breathing down her neck again. "I'm having a problem with Candy now. For the last two weeks she's closed the lines of communication between us . . . and I don't know why. One day we're fine, and the next, it's as if she were a stranger. I'm not sure what to do. Dr. Norris and I talk, and before I know it, the therapy session is over and I haven't said anything about Candy's behavior. Then I come home, and think Candy will be fine, and so another week passes. Maybe it's just called how to be a teenager. I don't know."

"Why don't you speak to Henry?" Marni asked. "I'm sure he'll give you some advice."

"That's a great idea," Nina said trying to encourage Kimberly. "He knew how to handle Don last night."

"That's true," Marni said. "You saw how understanding he could be. Call him Kim. I'll give you his telephone number."

"Henry?" Kimberly said. "Why didn't I think of that? He's a psychiatrist."

"Be careful," Nina warned. "It's not wise to have your therapist as your lover." Kimberly laughed, hesitantly at first and then more confidently. "See, you're feeling better already," Nina said. She tried to cover her social blunder.

"Speaking about sexual encounters," Marni said, "I'd love a private love nest. If I ever get lucky, it would be good to have a place where my kids can't walk in at any moment." She laughed. "What do you think?"

Two pair of eyes stared at Marni.

She meekly said, "It's the wine."

"I think it's a great idea," Nina cheered. "Why don't we create one? We do have a guest-house."

"That's obscene," Marni said, "but I'm tipsy enough to go for it. Some fresh air would revive us after all this food and wine." She got up from the sofa. "Why don't we brave the cold to check out the possibilities? Are you coming Kim?"

"I guess so," Kimberly said.

Walking out the front door, Marni said, "I want a heart-shaped jacuzzi." The cold ground crunched under her feet.

"Brr, it's freezing," Nina shivered. "An atrium with a hot tub would be ideal for a day like this."

They passed the pool, covered for the winter, and continued along the path.

"A sauna," Kimberly volunteered, "and a good stereo system. Music for lovers," Kimberly said laughingly.

"That's the spirit," Nina said to Kimberly. "Fun, fun, fun. Hey, did anyone bring the key?"

"I remembered," Marni said. "A smart real estate agent never forgets the keys. It could lose a sale." She was the first to enter the room. "Smells like a fire was made recently," Marni exclaimed, turning on the lights. "Did anyone ask Alex to do work on this place?" Marni looked directly at Nina.

"No," Nina said.

"Then what's this mattress on the floor," Marni said shaking her finger in Nina's direction. "Have you been holding out on us?"

"Honestly, it wasn't I," Nina answered. "I'm sorry I didn't think of it first. I can't imagine who, though."

"I know who it is," Kimberly said angrily not taking her eyes off the headband she held in her hand. "It's Candy."

Marni surprised by the tone of Kimberly's voice exchanged a look with Nina. "Don't jump to conclusions," Nina said. Once she heard Candy's name, it sobered her. "Kimberly, there's probably a reasonable explanation."

"I doubt it," Kimberly yelled racing out the door.

Chapter Seven

Kimberly threw open Candy's bedroom door and saw her daughter stretched out across the bed, reading. "You forgot something at the guest-house," Kimberly shouted hurling the headband and hitting Candy's cheek. "What do you have to say for yourself?" She wanted an immediate response. Candy rubbed the side of her face and sat up. "So, my memory isn't what it used to be, Mother," Candy replied still rubbing her face. "I must be getting older, or haven't you noticed?" Kimberly glared at her daughter for a few moments. "That's not an answer," she said in a more normal voice. "I am very well aware that you're getting older and you need your space. For the past few weeks you haven't been yourself. What's going on?"

"Mom, spare me. You're so busy with your new friends and work that you don't have time for me."

"That's not true, Candy. You're my priority, and you know that. I always have time for you but now, for some reason, you've shut me out. Talk to me, Candy. Please."

"Oh, get out of here. You're bothering me."

Kimberly took a few deep breaths. Finally, she said, "I'm not leaving, Candy. I'm your mother, not your enemy and don't you forget that. Why were you in the guest-house?"

"Why? You know why."

"You were with someone. Weren't you?"

Candy didn't answer.

"Your actions only harm yourself. You may want to strike out against me or your father. But Dr. Norris explained to you, you're the victim. Sure I'm upset as a mother. It makes me sick to my stomach especially since I'm part of the cause. But it's you who's harmed the most. I'm pleading with you. Please give yourself a chance. Please." Kimberly sat next Candy. All she wanted to do was embrace her and tell her everything will be all right. Kimberly started to touch her daughter's shoulder when she stopped in midair by her daughter's words, "I hate you." Frustrated, Kimberly slapped her daughter's cheek, the very spot already red.

"That's right, Mom," Candy said. "Hit me. I love it." She lifted her cheek closer. "Hit me again. I loved it last night."

"That's sick. Who was it?" Kimberly shouted, squeezing Candy's chin. "I want to know."

"It doesn't matter," Candy answered, pushing her hand away. "Someone was making me feel good because I let him. He wanted me, not you. Do you understand? Me."

Kimberly clasped her hands in her lap. Why did George get so drunk he didn't recognize Candy from me? She asked herself. "Why?" Kimberly looked at her daughter. She loved her so much. How could she have let this happen to Candy? "It was all my fault that we didn't leave your father sooner," Kimberly said trying to control her voice. "I'd do anything to take away the pain you feel. You were making such strides. Dr. Norris was helping us to sort out our feelings. I was looking forward to the move to Soundview. We worked together making this room just your space, a haven for you. Now this." She looked around the room. Remembering, Candy selected the earthy tone fabrics. Then she plotted a design on graph paper for draping the fabric along the eaves of the roofline. She wanted to create a valance around the perimeter of the room. Kimberly took pictures of the handiwork and told Candy this was to be the first exhibit in Candy's work portfolio. Her daughter was so happy. The second exhibit were pictures of the floral print bedspread and curtains to match the earth tones. Candy spent hours thumbing through fabric books until she chose the pattern. Proudly, Kimberly thought her daughter had a special eye for interior design. Each day after school they went to antique stores rummaging among old wood pieces.

They found chairs, tables, headboard and desk for Candy's bedroom and sitting room. Kimberly believed her life was finally on course during the time she and Candy spent together. They were always talking and laughing. "What happened?" she said softly. Kimberly waited for her daughter's response. The second hand on the alarm clock ticked off the seconds. Kimberly grew impatient. Finally, she grabbed Candy's shoulders and shouted into her face, "Tell me, Candy, I want to know! Tell me! Tell me!" Candy started to cry. Kimberly slid her arms around to Candy's back and felt her daughter's body shudder with sobs. She held her tightly, trying to soothe her. "I saw Dad," Candy said after several minutes.

"You what," Kimberly exclaimed through clenched teeth, pushing Candy from her. "I told him I would have him thrown in jail if he ever came near you again. I'm not interested in his apologies to you or his excuses he was too drunk to know that it wasn't me. I want him to stay away from you. That's it. Permanently." Kimberly took hold of Candy's shoulders again wanting to impress on her she meant what she said. "Every time you see him, you act out—first the drugs, then the boys. Now what Candy? You must promise not to see him again. You can't handle it."

"But Mom. . . ."

"Respect my wishes. That's all I'm asking. He'll only destroy what we're trying to build together." Kimberly released her daughter's shoulders and looked around the room stopping at the free standing mirror. She saw her father's angry face. "Damn you," she mouthed at the image reflected in the glass. Her mind whirled with hateful thoughts. I'm still cursed for moving to New York against your wishes. Why are you so mean and evil? Will you ever stop? Did you have to send George to do your dirty work? He ruined our marriage, our lives, and look what he did to Candy. I didn't commit a sin by leaving home, I just wanted to be a architect. Why can't you understand that." She took a deep breath. "I'm calling Dr. Norris," she said softly to Candy. "We'll see her tomorrow." Kimberly put her arm around Candy's shoulders, kissing her cheek where the headband landed. She knew that she had to get rid of the evil threat or it would always be lurking in some dark cloud waiting to strike them at any moment.

Chapter Eight

Before undressing, Marni turned on the shower allowing time for the water to get hot. The heat would be soothing. She was expecting Paul for dinner in two hours. It was a perfect evening to entertain at home. Greg was visiting a camp buddy for the weekend and Neil had a slumber party.

Marni was looking forward to the evening. It was only one week since the house warming gala. Her sudden display of feelings for Paul other than her usual friendly demeanor troubled her. She wondered if it was just a needy move since her agreement between Don and herself was settled. Did she flip for the first man who found her attractive? Was she afraid to be alone? Hadn't she been alone emotionally for a long time? She dropped each of her garments on the floor as the steam slowly filled the room, gradually wrapping her in an opaque mist. She stepped into the shower stall, adjusted the water temperature, took the shower head unit in her hand, and set the spray to gentle massage. Her tenseness started to melt away. Slowly, she ran the pulsating stream across the nape of her neck and down her shoulders, her olive skin took on a pinkish tone. The aches started to disappear. The spray oscillated on her tender breasts, stimulating her nipples. She closed her eyes, surrendering herself to the sensation and began envisioning a faceless man, obscure in the vapor, except his erect manhood beckoning to her. Her body simulated imagined rhythms. She responded with the spray directed at the joining of her inner thighs. Features appeared on the faceless man. It was Paul. Her muscles tensed. She replaced the shower head unit.

Marni swung open her door at seven thirty and Paul greeted her with a bouquet of red roses. "They're beautiful," Marni said while his smile melted her insides. "Thanks." She liked the way he looked in casual clothes—a brown and white argyle sweater and tan chinos. Marni didn't usually see him dressed in this way. "My pleasure," Paul replied. "What smells so good?" Marni watched him raise his head and breathe deeply. "I'm baking bread." She purposely timed her bread machine so that the strongest baking aromas would be when Paul arrived. "I can't wait to taste it," he said. Marni shrugged her shoulders, "Sorry," she said. "It won't be ready for a while." She headed toward the kitchen holding the flowers but stopped in front of the block glass wall. "Paul, what are you drinking?" she asked. "We're having wine with dinner."

"Water with lemon," he answered.

A few minutes later Marni was centering the vase of flowers on a narrow black metal table behind the sofa where Paul was sitting. "There," she said. "I can enjoy them from any place in the room." Then she put down two glasses of water and a bowl of chips on the cocktail table. "Come join me," he said. "In a second," she responded on her way to the fireplace. "I want to get a better fire going."

"Very quiet for two boys to be living here," Paul said.

"They're away, visiting friends," Marni said, adding another log and immediately sparking a flame. "I had no interruptions during the preparation of dinner."

"Then it better be good." Paul lifted his drink as Marni sat down. She touched hers with his. "To health," she said. "At least through dinner," Paul said. "And you're getting a good one," Marni quickly responded. "I'm a woman of my word." She thumbed through her collection of recipes that required little preparation, tasted good, and looked well on the plate. You needed this kind of file when you were working and still liked to entertain. "Do I detect a guilty expression on your face?" Marni asked. Paul didn't answer. "Don't be," she said. "I enjoy cooking. Anyhow, it was my turn to treat you to dinner. You've taken me to dinner twice this week." She really needed this quiet time with Paul to sort out her feelings.

"You have a choice of the next restaurant," Paul said.

"How do you know there'll be a next time?" Marni drank

some water from her glass. "Maybe what's taking place has to do with the divorce. It could just be my reaction."

"I don't think so. We know each other pretty well. You have many traits I admire. You're understanding and compassionate. Something I saw when my wife died. It meant a great deal to hear your voice on the telephone pushing me to get on with my life." Hearing all of this, Marni was feeling uncomfortable. Offhandedly, she said, "What are friends for?" She touched his arm lightly. "You're intelligent," he said. "Self-motivated." She couldn't believe Paul went on. "Good business sense. Not a manipulative individual unless you're trying to make a deal. That kind of behavior is justifiable." Marni laughed. "Maybe I should run for office," she said. "With all those superlatives, you can be my campaign manager. Actually, I live in the community," Marni explained. "It's important to be able to walk in the food store with my head up."

"I can appreciate that."

"Do you remember the first closing we had together?" Marni asked. "My stomach was filled with fluttering butterflies. The commission check was my trophy as a novice real estate person."

"I know," he said. "It was up to me to make sure there was a smooth closing process. It was the initiation of my own law office. I also needed the fee for rent."

"A start for both of us," Marni said lightheartedly.

"Let's drink to that," Paul said moving closer to Marni. "Are you hungry?" she asked. She hated to get up but she needed to finish the cooking of the meal. "Starving," Paul said rubbing his stomach.

"Enjoy the fire. Give me a few minutes."

After a while, Marni came out of the kitchen and lit two red tapered candles resting in low cube-like crystal holders.

"What can I do?" Paul asked from the couch.

"Follow me," Marni answered waving her hand.

Paul carried out two glass bowls filled with caesar salad and the freshly baked rye bread on a lucite cutting board. Marni followed. She carried two dinner plates of swordfish steak lightly covered with a soy sauce sprinkled with green onions, a mound of rice pilaf and a wedge of lemon. She placed the dinner plates on the table. Then she took off her apron revealing a red turtle neck sweater and black pin-stripe pants. She blended perfectly with the decor of her living area. "Bon appetit," she said sitting. "This looks wonderful," Paul said reaching for the wine bottle. "Let me open this." Marni looked at the hi-lights and left the table long enough to turn them off. They dined by the light of the luminous fireplace and flickering candles, a sense of comfort passed between Marni and Paul.

"Quite a romantic setting," Paul said pouring the wine. Marni smiled. "I told you that I had a thing for entertaining like this." She looked around the room—the burning fireplace, the flowers on the table, and the glassware glistening in the candlelight. Her efforts to create something special paid off. She would never have guessed that she would have had someone so wonderful to share it. "You're my first guest here, Paul."

"I hope the first of many more dinners to come," Paul said quickly. "Where did you learn to cook?"

"Cookbooks. My mother. My grandmother. By the way, how's your Mother?" Marni asked. "I didn't see her at our last MADD chapter meeting."

"She's fine. Living in Florida for the winter months. I hear my mother's voice on my answering machine all the time. She fills the tape with numbers of women that she meets in various places. Her motive is to get her son married."

"You're what the women would say, some catch," Marni said laughingly. "What would you say?" Paul asked. Marni felt her cheeks become hot and wondered if they were bright red. "I would agree. You're quite a catch."

"Then we'll continue dating?"

"Yes. We will." Marni drank some wine and then said to Paul, "You haven't seen my bitchy side yet."

"Yes I have. Have you forgotten I'm your lawyer?"

"Okay, personal stuff," she put some swordfish on her fork.

"I'm moody sometimes," he answered. "That'll cancel each other's less than splendid moments. Is this confession time?" She shook her head. "Not really," she answered. "Good," Paul responded. "I want to learn about you first hand." She knew that she could be a real head case sometimes but she thought who wasn't. I am who I am, she said to herself, but she could adapt to someone else if there was reason.

"We're such good friends," Marni said smoothing her hair behind her ears, "and have a really good business relationship. I don't want to mess it up." She really didn't. "We won't," Paul assured her. "We're adults." Marni couldn't tell Paul that she liked his face across the table. Softly she said, "It could be part of something wonderful." Paul raised his glass. "That's what I want to hear." She started to believe that also.

Marni served espresso in the den to complete the dinner. Afterwards she settled herself close to Paul on the sofa using his out stretched arm for a pillow. They watched the movie Casablanca. She had it in her video collection of old movies. Throughout the rest of the evening, she continued to feel his nearness comforting. It helped her to relax although her body was astir from her head down to her tiny toe. When it was time for Paul to leave, she allowed herself to be drawn into his arms. Her lips pressed against his.

Stepping out the door, he said to her, "When do I see you again? What about tomorrow?"

"I have an appointment to show a property in the morning. How about lunch?" Marni saw his great smile again. "I'll call you at the office." She was already thinking where they should go.

Chapter Nine

As Kimberly neared La Trieste's green canopied entryway, she smelled the savory aroma of continental cuisine and for a split second she forgot why she was there. Pulling open the door she faced Henry taking off his coat. "Hello," she said. A quick glance around. "Good to see you again," he replied flipping his coat over his arm. Some of her trepidation eased with his greeting. He helped Kimberly off with her coat, then checked both garments. She walked over to the empty reception desk looking for Victorio. Noticing him in the middle of the dining room, she waved. She was glad that she chose this restaurant. It had a certain mellow ambience with light colored walls and pastel paintings of gardens in full bloom.

"He's good about honoring reservations," Henry said now standing next to her. "I'm sure our table is ready." Kimberly already noticed empty ones. "Here he comes," she said.

"Hello, Senora Mathews. Hello, Dr. Gordon," Victorio said moving around the reception desk. He scanned the reservation book, took two menus and said, "Follow me." They maneuvered past several filled tables stopping at a corner table. Kimberly slipped into the chair that Victorio was holding. She picked up her napkin and placed it on her lap, fiddling with its edges.

"Would you like a drink Senora?" Victorio asked.

"A Bloody Mary, please," Kimberly said. "The spicier the better." Now that she was sitting with Henry she was too nervous to tell him anything.

"And you Senor?"

"A Perrier, please."

"How's the bank building going?" Henry asked. Kimberly was somewhat glad for the small talk to break the ice. "Great," she said. "We finally got our last approval. I can't wait to start construction." Almost at once she realized that she was too upset to have a socialable conversation. "Oh, Henry I didn't come here to talk about my work. I need some advice." She was desperate for all the help she could get since her recent confrontation with Candy.

"I'll try and help you in anyway I can. Whenever you're comfortable, I'm ready to listen."

Kimberly took a deep breath. "Let me give you some background," she said. "I moved to New York to start a new life. In one year I found a good job and met George, my ex-husband. I was ecstatic. He was perfect for me. He cared about pleasing me and my happiness was very important to him. I thought we had a storybook romance, a reward to make up for my miserable childhood. God was sending me a signal, defying my father's parting gift to me, his curse."

"Kimberly, there's no such thing as a curse," Henry said frowning.

"That's what my therapist, Dr. Norris says, also. I'm not convinced," Kimberly said. "My father never wanted me to come to New York. He was a reverend. He paid for my education so that one day I could design churches for him all over the country. Until then, he expected me to remain at home, marry someone he chose, and propagate the species. He said I had to set an example for the congregants. I never received his blessing to leave. He wouldn't listen when I told him that staying home meant wasting the talent God gave me. I'll never forget our last words."

"Excuse me," Victorio said, "your drinks." Victorio placed them on the table. "Thank you," said Henry. Then he leaned toward the table, "Now what were you going to say?" he asked Kimberly.

Kimberly took another deep breath. "We were standing in his church office. It was cold and the light was dim. He told me if I left he would disown me. I told him that I'll pay that price." Henry shrugged his shoulders. "That doesn't sound much like a curse," Henry said. "There's more," Kimberly murmured, taking a gulp from her Bloody Mary. "Pointing his finger at my heart he told me God would punish me."

"How did you answer him?" Henry asked softly.

"His words made me so angry," she said raising her voice. "I yelled back that God had punished me already. He gave me him for my father." Embarrassed, Kimberly looked around to see if anyone heard her. She hoped everyone was too busy with their own conversation. In a quieter tone she continued. "That's when my father went ballistic." Henry gripped the sides of the table with his hand. "Did he strike you?" he asked. "I didn't give him the chance. I ran out of the church as fast as my feet would take me. All he could do was throw his books and shout repeatedly, God will punish me."

"I know that it must have sounded very threatening, perhaps even diabolical but your father was only human like the rest of us. He didn't put a curse on you."

"Wait I'm not finished. "It was my wedding night. George and I were awakened by the ringing of the phone. George answered it. It was my roommate. My parents' plane crashed on the way to an evangelical meeting. I didn't go to their funeral. I allowed the family lawyer to take care of all the matters."

"That was a coincidence. These things happen. Some kids have the misfortune to have parents who have no right to be parents," Henry said covering Kimberly's hand with his own. "You were one of them."

Kimberly closed her eyes holding back the tears. "It's more than just that," she said encouraged by Henry's gesture to go on. "My father molested me. I"m still working out the effects with Dr. Norris, my therapist." Henry rubbed his bearded chin. "That's a rough beginning being part of a dysfunctional family."

"Don't I know it?" said Kimberly. "You might think my father didn't have some power to throw a curse on me but I think he did. George was his messenger." She paused for more of her drink. "George and I didn't have a good marriage. It was complicated by my upbringing and his many problems, which I didn't know about at the time of our marriage. He was an alcoholic. Three years ago I finally decided to divorce him but it took me a year to work up my courage. I arrived home from the office and George was drinking but he was always drinking so I didn't put off telling him my decision. I simply said I was leaving him. He told me how much he needed me and I told him he needed only his bottle. It became a shouting match until he grabbed me and started slapping me around."

"How terrible," Henry said. He rubbed his hand across his bearded cheek and chin.

"I tried to protect myself and wanted to call Dr. Freemont, George's doctor. When George heard the doctor's name, he became more abusive and shouted he didn't need any sedatives or lectures. All he wanted was me." Kimberly stopped speaking before she could tell about her "ides of March." She took a few deep breaths. The words poured out of her, the gush bringing with it the anguish of a living hell. "Henry," she said, "what happened to Candy and me that day is seared into my being. He tried to kiss my clenched lips, and in anger he threw me down onto the floor. I tried to get away but George caught me and pinned me down, ripping off my clothes and then his. I was paralyzed with fear." She twisted the corner of the napkin in her lap. "He forced my legs apart and fell on top of me. I punched his face with my fists but he grabbed my hands and kept thrusting himself deeper and deeper into me. The pain pierced my body and I prayed for it to be over. It took him a long time to come because he was so drunk. Afterwards without saying a word he dressed and left the house. When I heard George's car leaving the driveway, I crawled to my clothes. There was blood dripping down my legs. I called Dr. Bader's office, my gynecologist, and then a cab. Dr. Bader was a sympathetic listener and supported my decision to separate from George. She was the one who suggested I contact Dr. Norris, a family psychologist to help Candy and myself through the trying time."

"That was a wise move," Henry said. "It was," Kimberly responded while mixing her drink with a straw. "Is there more to the story?" Henry asked. Kimberly nodded and then began speaking.

"When I returned from the doctor's office, the cab pulled up next to George's car. Opening the front door, I heard incoherent noises coming from upstairs. I called out Candy's name but there was no answer. As I climbed the stairs, the sounds became louder. They were coming from my bedroom. Standing in the doorway, I saw George. He was naked from the waist down, his body was on top of someone whose legs were kicking his stomach. He tried to stop the movement by using his hands to push the legs flat under him. I screamed something. His face was pressed against the pillow protecting himself from clawing nails. I heard him slur my name. Then my heart stopped beating when I heard Candy say, "Daddy . . . no . . . please . . . I'm not Mommy." An empty liquor bottle was next to the bed. I picked it up and clobbered George's head with it. It took all my strength to move his body off Candy. Once free she rolled into a ball. I grabbed her arm and dragged her out of the house. Closing the front door behind us there wasn't a concern if George was dead. You see what I'm saying. My father sent him to punish me." She finished her drink and looked across to Henry.

"Kimberly," Henry said softly, "George was a troubled human being, unfortunately you married him. You were afraid to leave him because being alone in the world can be frightening. All quite understandable. It's not a curse. There's a reason for everything."

"That's what you say but I'm not convinced." It was the same words she heard from Dr. Norris often. "Let's just talk about Candy now." She saw Henry nod, acquiescing to her wishes. "Whatever you want Kimberly," he said. "I'm here to listen." She was grateful for that. "Anyway," she began again, "I really tried to help Candy right away. We started seeing Dr. Norris. I have a restraining order to keep George away but it means nothing. He still manages to see her. Each time he has told her how sorry he was. He was drunk. Afterwards she has acted out with drugs and boys. Candy didn't see George for months. He was in rehab. During that time, Dr. Norris helped her work out her feelings. She started getting good marks in school again and participating in school functions. Feeling good about herself, Candy stopped therapy. What could I say? She was doing fine. Candy saw George a few weeks ago and it affected her behavior all over again. She probably should have continued seeing Dr. Norris all along. This whole thing breaks my heart." Kimberly's eyes became watery; her lips quivered. "I want to kill him," she said. "George has no right to keep coming back into her life and my life."

Henry reached across the table and gently placed her face between his hands. He spoke to her in a low, soothing voice. "You have reason for your anger, but I want you to promise me something." He raised her face. "Look at me, Kimberly. Listen to what I am saying. Promise me," he said, "you won't act on those raw emotions. It's not in your interest or Candy's. Those kinds of feelings get you into trouble." Kimberly slowly nodded. Then she held Henry's hands in place for a few moments. She found strength from his touch. His eyes told her that she had found someone who truly cared. "What'll happen to Candy?" she lamented.

"You brought her through a crisis before with therapy, and you can do it again. Candy needs help sorting out her feelings for her father, for you, and more importantly how she feels about herself. It might be necessary to have joint therapy—and I mean with all three of you."

"I can't, Henry," Kimberly said abruptly moving back in her seat. "Dr. Norris said I should do that, too. That's asking too much of me."

"It might be the only way Candy can get the past behind her. You have the love and strength to do whatever it takes to help her. I can feel that from you. I believe in her future and yours."

"Please don't give me false hope, Henry." She wanted so much to believe everything would be all right. "Kimberly, I've been a psychiatrist for twenty-five years and feel almost anything is possible, as long as people are willing to try."

"Candy did agree to go back into therapy," Kimberly said.

"Good," he said. "That's the first step. If you'd like, I can stop by the house and meet Candy. I can also speak to Dr. Norris with your permission." Henry was a blurred image through Kimberly's teary eyes. "Yes," she said to Henry, "I would appreciate that. Your support makes me feel better. Thank you." It was Kimberly's second time in her life that she had the sympathetic ear of a man willing to help her. The other one was Dr. Freemont but she never felt as comfortable as she was feeling right now.

Chapter Ten

"Mmmmm . . . what smells so good?" Kimberly asked. She was surprised to see Candy standing next to the kitchen stove. Her daughter was busily stirring something in Kimberly's favorite sauce pan. "I'm making fettucini bolognese," Candy replied. "We're having company for dinner, Marni and Nina. I asked Greg and Neil but they didn't want to come." Kimberly put her briefcase down on the kitchen table. She knew making dinner for people involved alot of preparation and was willing to help although Candy seemed to have everything under control. "Do you want me to do anything?" Kimberly asked. "Nope, I'm doing fine," Candy answered. "I have your recipe card to follow." Kimberly watched Candy add some olive oil. "In that case I'll take off my shoes and watch you from my chair. What's the occasion?"

"I said some really mean things to you a few weeks ago," Candy replied continuing to stir. "I wanted to make it up to you." Kimberly was surprised. "There was a reason for your behavior," she said softly. "I'm your mother. I understand. How come Marni and Nina?"

"Well . . . they knew I was in the guest-house and you were angry about it. It's my way of showing them I'm not all bad." Candy opened the door of the oak cabinet above her head and reached for a jar of oregano.

"Listen Candy, Nina understands how teenage girls can act sometimes. She was never a wilting flower, so to speak. You heard about that, the night we had dinner together. She's had a lively past. Marni is a parent and knows kids aren't perfect. Listen if you were perfect what would I do. Right?"

"Oh, Mom, you've been there for me."

"Not always Candy but I'm trying now. Really trying. Turn around a second, hon. Someone has a new hairdo."

"Do you like it?"

"Weren't you just getting a trim?"

"Andre' permed it for me," Candy said running her hand through her hair. "What do you think?"

"Very flattering. I bet no maintenance. Wash it and let it dry naturally."

"Yep," Candy said nonchalantly.

"What did Bonita do all that time?"

Kimberly wanted to know. She had given Bonita strict instructions not to let Candy out of her sight for one minute. "Bonita didn't mind waiting for me. In fact, she got a hair-cut and manicure." Kimberly immediately decided to reimburse Bonita or she would have no money left from Kimberly's payment for her driving services.

"She's a good person and so are you." Candy walked over to her mother holding the mixing spoon in the air and planted a kiss on her cheek. "I'm so excited about my new look."

"My, my," Kimberly said returning her daughter's kiss. "It sounds like you had a good day today."

"I did. Dr. Norris and I had a super session." Candy said walking back to the stove.

"If you'd care to," Kimberly said choosing her words, "I'd love to hear about it." She turned her chair around to fully face Candy.

"Okay. Well . . . Dr. Norris asked me if I felt I had changed since I started going to her office. What is it, Mom? Two years ago?"

"That sounds about right."

"Well, she really made me think about myself with that question. There was a change. No more drugs. School work completed on time. Participation in school functions. Didn't I stop seeing her because I thought I was okay? Then I did something stupid. Why?"

"I've watched you change and I'm very proud of you. We know why you acted out."

"I should've handled seeing Dad and not freak out. Then I took it out on you and me. It's not right. I've got to control myself."

"I can't think rationally about him either," Kimberly said taking a deep breath. "Some demon takes over."

"Dr. Norris is going to help me. She's says if I work at it I'll be okay." Candy placed a cover on the sauce pan and turned to face her mother. "It's a relief to know I'm curable."

"Then promise me you won't shut me out again. I really want to help you too. I love you. You're my daughter."

"I'll try and that's all Dr. Norris wanted to hear. She said it's not good to make promises you might have trouble keeping."

"I guess I'll have to accept that. Is that the reason for the new hairdo?"

"When I was sitting in Andre's chair, he asked me what I wanted done. It felt right to make a complete change so I said to Andre, "Go for it. Here I am." Candy twirled around. "The new me." Kimberly was relieved with her daughter's better feeling of herself. She almost felt that maybe now she would beat this evil threat to her and Candy's happiness. "I love the new you and the old one too."

"Thanks, Mom," Candy said. "You know, I bet Dad won't recognize me." Kimberly sat straighter in her chair. "He better not attempt to see you again. I called Dr. Freemont and asked him to speak to your father. Hopefully, he'll listen this time with rehab and all." Kimberly depended on Dr. Freemont during times like this and George usually listened to the doctor.

"If I do see Dad, maybe I can handle it. I'm going to try." Kimberly hoped her relationship was such that Candy would tell her of the meeting. She really wanted to be there for her daughter and not repeat her mother's mistakes by ignoring her father's behavior. Kimberly was left on her own to deal with the mistreatment. "I want to help you Candy. All I can."

Kimberly stood up. "When is dinner?" Kimberly asked remembering Marni and Nina were coming. "In about twenty minutes," Candy said cutting a cucumber. "Just enough time for me to change." Kimberly started to leave the room but reconsidered. She walked to her daughter and gave her a hug. Life was frightening sometimes, she thought, but then there were the good moments. Thank god for them.

The doorbell rang just as Kimberly came down the stairs in a blue work shirt and a pair of jeans. "I'll get it," she called out to Candy.

Nina was standing under the portico holding a seltzer bottle and a jar of chocolate syrup. "I brought the makings of dessert," she said to Kimberly.

"Your father's specialty, an egg cream. I can't wait." Nina held up the ingredients and said, "None other." Kimberly wasn't really jumping for joy when she heard there were dinner guests. She was tired and she wanted to spend time with Candy. Now that Nina walked in with the fixings for an egg cream, she was glad that her daughter arranged the dinner party.

"Hold the door open," Marni said racing across the courtyard. "Take your time," Kimberly answered. She let Marni walk by her then she closed the door. "What did you bring?" she asked Marni, noticing a shopping bag. "Italian bread and Tiramisu."

"This is going to be some dinner," Kimberly declared. She was pleased by the women's response to Candy's reaching out. "Hang your coats in the closet so we can get to the food."

"Hi," Candy said taking the bread out of the bag. "I need this for garlic bread. Thanks for picking it up for me."

"Candy," Nina said, "how does egg creams and Tiramisu sound for dessert. I hope it goes with your menu?"

"Wow," Candy replied. "Are you nuts? That's great with anything. I can't wait."

"You're making egg creams?" Marni said to Nina. "Hey, what about a BLT?" Marni laughed. "You're really a smart ass, ya' know," Nina retorted. "Let's take this act on the road," Kimberly said thinking she always felt happier when the women were around. "Follow me." She led the laughing twosome through a hallway to the kitchen where she immediately placed the dessert items in the refrigerator.

"Whatever you're cooking smells wonderful," Nina said to Candy lifting the cover of the sauce pan. "Too many cooks in here," Candy said taking the cover out of Nina's hand. "Go sit in the dining room. The table is set."

"Come on, Nina," Marni said opening the double doors to the dining room. The heat from the burning fireplace unexpectedly hit her face. "You have a great fire going, Candy," Marni said turning toward the kitchen. Candy holding a bowl of salad came alongside her. "I know you guys always make one when you're in the library," she said. "That's very thoughtful," Kimberly said to her daughter.

"Furniture came," Marni exclaimed realizing the dining room was no longer an empty space. "Cherrywood set looks great in here." Kimberly reassured herself with a quick glance around. "Thanks," she answered. "God knows it took long enough to be delivered. Go look in the living room and tell me what you think." Kimberly followed Marni into the room. She was anxious for Marni's opinion. She knew that Marni had a good eye for design. "I love your fabrics," Marni said slowly perusing the country French motif making up the room. Kimberly was relieved to hear Marni's praise. "I was hesitant to use celery green and magenta," Kimberly said, "but it's a good combination." Marni made a pirouette movement to inspect the room again, "Smashing," she said. "I told you this wing was made for you." Kimberly crossed her fingers hoping that Marni was right.

"It means alot to me to have my own place," Kimberly said. "It's tough renting. You're afraid something will spill on the upholstery or a vase will break. It's not comfortable." Marni shrugged. "It served its purpose," she said. "It gave you a chance to find this place." Kimberly thought that was true.

"Am I the only one eating?" Nina called from the dining room.

"We're coming," Marni replied. "Be happy, Kimberly," she said squeezing Kimberly's arm. "Enjoy it." Kimberly put her hand over Marni's and said softly, "I'm trying." Marni and Kimberly joined Nina. They pushed their chairs toward the dining room chairs as Candy put on the table a glass bowl filled with pasta and a basket of garlic bread.

"The salad is delicious. The anchovies make it," Nina said. "By the way I like your new hairdo Candy. Permed it, right?" Candy made a face. "A smelly one, too," she said. Nina fluffed up her hair. "My wave is natural. Some women with wavy hair straighten it," Nina said. "Me, the wilder the better."

"Is that just your hair?" Marni said. Then she thought about Candy and realized this wasn't the time to instigate Nina.

"Well, I like adventure," Nina replied. "It's fun to throw all caution to the wind." When the words left her lips, Nina wanted to obliterate them with a bomb. She rolled her eyes so Marni could see that she made a mistake. Marni started it and she finished it. How fitting? How dumb can one get, Nina thought.

"Do you ever get hurt?" Candy asked Nina.

"What do you mean by hurt?" Nina asked. "Physically? Mentally?"

"Both," Candy said.

"I never hurt myself physically. Why inflict pain on myself? As I grow older my actions seem not to have the excitement they once held for me. It's probably called growing up, looking for something meaningful in my life." Nina wasn't just doing damage control by her statement but she was beginning to feel this. Each day the feeling grew stronger.

"Yeah," Candy said. "I can understand that."

"I like to be in control of my life," Marni said thinking about Candy in the guest-house. "It's less stressful. God knows, I get plenty of stress in the office."

"I know what you mean," Kimberly said. "The office can be grueling but I do everything possible to create an atmosphere to eliminate the big S factor. Most of the time it works. My personal life . . . is another story. Some things are ruled by an evil spirit. It's difficult to combat."

"Evil spirit," Nina said. "Voodoo. That's ridiculous."

"Not like that," Kimberly said. "There are Godly spirits and some are evil."

"The spirit of God is supposed to make you feel good," Marni said.

"I guess," Kimberly said. She breathed deeply. "I just don't feel that way."

"Is that what happens when your father is a reverend?" Nina asked.

"He was a dominate force in my life and my mother's. Whatever we did had to be sanctioned by him and God."

"I would have driven him crazy," Nina said.

"He wouldn't have given you the opportunity, Nina."

"My father let me do anything I wanted," Marni interjected, "as long as my mother said it was okay. The house was her domain."

"That sounds like a normal upbringing," Kimberly said. "I wish it were mine."

"If I didn't think my parents would approve," Nina said, "I didn't tell them. It made my life easier but thinking about it now it was the wrong thing to do. Thank God, it was lucky I had the best father in the world. Pops told me that he knew about my past shenanigans when I asked him permission to study at the Sorbonne. It was silly of me to think some neighbor wouldn't have said something. The whole frigging neighborhood came into the candy store. But Pops came through for me anyway, he gave me his approval over the objections of my mother."

"You're lucky, too," Kimberly said thinking too bad she had her father and then George. "Pops sounds special." She was having too good a time to remember her depressing past. She wouldn't let those memories take hold of her tonight.

"This dinner was special," Marni said to Candy. "From beginning to end," Nina added. "It was, wasn't it?" Kimberly proudly said. "My daughter is a culinary whiz." Kimberly was glad she had the opportunity to show off Candy and she owed it all to her daughter. She had to make sure that she thanked her when Marni and Nina left. "Since the evening worked out," Candy said, "I might do it again." Kimberly hearing what Candy said, thought maybe her move to Soundview might turn out all right. Candy was on the right track again and Kimberly had a support team now. Something that was missing in the past.

Chapter Eleven

The late afternoon sun filtered through the blinds, warming Marni's fingers tapping on the computer keyboard. She had been inserting all kinds of number combinations in the lotus program to see the potential of a construction project. The ringing of her private phone interrupted her chain of thought. "Hello," she answered. Her tone revealed that she was annoyed to be disturbed. "Hi, Marni," Paul's voice immediately changed her mood. She was glad it was him. "How's your day going?"

"Unfortunately, very delayed," said Paul. "I have to cancel our theater plans."

"Too bad. Then I won't see you tonight?"

"I'm not cancelling our evening just the tickets. I don't know exactly how long this meeting will last, but it would be past curtain time. My client wants to make up for the delay. He knows I have a date with this dynamite woman, so he arranged something special for us. We have a suite for the weekend at the Plaza Hotel. Is that a fair substitution?"

Marni did not respond. She told him already that she didn't want to rush into anything. So far, it was lunch, dinner, tennis or a movie ending with a good night kiss. There was no pressure to go to bed with him. She was now confronted with a decision that was inevitable. Her present state of mind was in total denial. "What's the matter?" Paul asked. "I thought you would be enthusiastic." Her innuendos during their conversations and her response when they kissed would give him that feeling. How could she blame him for his suggestion? However she couldn't commit on the telephone, either. It would take a while for her to be intimate again. "I don't know, Paul. Let me think about it."

"Whatever you say," Paul said. "How about this. We take advantage of the setting and have a dinner for two, overlooking Central Park." Marni was grateful for his understanding. "I'd like that," Marni said. "A late evening won't be a problem. The kids have plans with my parents for the weekend. What time do you think you'll get there?"

"I can't answer that, but I'm not far from the hotel. Once the meeting is over, I'll jump into a cab. The suite is ours now. Come into the city whenever you want."

"I'll be waiting for you," Marni said softly. "Good luck with the meeting."

"Thanks. I can't wait to see you. Drive carefully."

Marni returned to her paperwork. After awhile, she achieved her goal and figured out a way for the deal to work. She printed the numbers. At five o'clock, she left her office. There was no rushing for carpools or the kids dinner. Her parents had picked up the boys from their schools. Leisurely she inspected the clothes in her closet. Holding a few silk shirts against her it was still tough making a decision. She glanced at the overnight case sitting on the floor. I knew this time would eventually come, she thought. Am I ready? Won't there always be an uncertainty going along with that first time with Paul? Isn't it normal? She packed a few essential for a stay over promising herself she would see what happens.

Dressing in front of the mirror she was about to slip into a black lace teddy but stopped. Leaning toward the glass she studied her face from every angle. There were no aging lines. "I look the same," she said to herself. "It's the same me looking out of the same brown eyes for the last thirty-eight years." She turned around scanning her nakedness. Her deep olive skin was still taut around her narrow frame, but there was enough softness to her curves to leave no doubt about her sensuality. After pulling up the teddy, she finished dressing. For the last time she checked her appearance in the mirror. The custom fit of her taupe suit was perfect. She straightened her bangs and was ready for whatever was to happen.

Marni arrived at the Plaza, car-weary from the city-bound traffic, a hazard of living in the suburbs of New York. She checked in at the front desk and immediately received the VIP treatment. An assistant manager escorted her to the suite while a smartly uniformed bellhop carried her luggage. As the door swung open to the suite, Marni inspected the surroundings. A sitting room was tastefully decorated with French reproductions of the Eighteenth Century. The upholstered seating was in a bright blue. Resting on the coffee table was a silver champagne bucket filled with a magnum of Dom Perignon and a vase of red roses. She unpinned the card. It said, "How do you like it so far? P." A wave of goose bumps rippled through her in anticipation. Marni was glad she had packed a few sexy things. The manager drew open the drapes, revealing a spectacular view of Central Park at night. Although Marni was a regular visitor to New York, she became a tourist filled with awe seeing the city's skyline. "May I open the champagne for you, Madam?" the bellhop asked, having just put her suitcase in the bedroom. Marni reluctantly pulled herself away from the window. "Yes, please," she replied. When the hotel staff finally departed, she enjoyed her champagne. The bubbles tickled her nose. She inspected the suite and ended the tour in the bedroom—spacious for New York and duplicating the color design and elegance of the sitting room. She twirled around, laughing aloud. She stopped near the open door of the bathroom. The all-marble room, with a huge sunken tub surrounded with mirrors, was too tempting for her to resist. She turned on the gold faucets and ran the water, pouring in all the complimentary packets of bubble bath.

Returning to the bedroom, she unpacked, hung up her clothes, including the ones she had been wearing, and slipped on her robe. While waiting for the tub to fill, she turned on the radio. The voice of Frank Sinatra singing "Nice and Easy" resounded from the speaker. She brought the champagne bucket into the bedroom, refilled her glass, and went to check the bath. It was perfect. She placed her glass on the ledge of the tub. Then she wrapped a rubber band around the ends of her hair, stepped out of the robe and into the invigorating heat of the water. A cloud of bubbles engulfed her as she thought life was wonderful.

Marni didn't know how long Paul had been standing there,

watching her. She felt a presence, or perhaps heard his breathing. She opened her eyes slowly and there he was in the doorway. Leaning on the frame, he was dressed in a robe. Paul held a glass of champagne in one hand and a red rose in the other. A flush spread across her body as Paul approached her. He placed the rose between her breasts, raised his glass and said, "Its beauty pales next to yours." Marni laughed and clinked Paul's glass with her own, looking up at him invitingly. "Join me," she said.

"Just what I need after the kind of day I had."

She watched Paul undo his robe and hang it on the door. His body was lean barely showing any sign of his forty-three years. He climbed into the tub, easing his body beneath the warm, soporific water. A cocoon of serenity blanketed them as they lay silently suspended in a moire of effervescence. After awhile, Marni turned toward Paul and ran her fingers through the hairs of his chest, familiarizing herself with the feel of his skin. Then she placed her hand behind Paul's head and massaged his tight neck muscles. He closed his eyes, pretending to rest, but Marni suddenly felt an odd sensation along her left side. Paul was tickling her. She tried to squelch her giggling. "Paul, stop that," she said laughingly. He innocently asked, "Stop what?" She cried through her laughter, "Paul, please," and the water churned with her squirming motions but Paul didn't stop. Marni caught her breath and, in a desperate move, placed her hands on his head and pushed him under the water. She was instantly grabbed by Paul and pulled under with him. They came up for air, water streaming down their bodies, arms wrapped tightly around each other, kissing fully on the lips. She pushed him away. "Look what you've done to my hair," she admonished playfully.

Marni hopped out of the tub. Paul's eyes watched admiringly as she toweled off and then annoited herself with oil, enhancing her skin with a sensual luster. Soon after, Paul climbed out of the tub, took the towel she handed to him, and slipped it around her, pulling her toward him and holding her closely. "You feel so good," he said. He dried her leisurely. She relished the sensuality of it. Then Paul quickly dried himself and flipped the towel over the edge of the bath tub. With ease, he swooped

Marni into his arms and carried her into the bedroom, throwing back the velvet coverlet and lowering her onto the bed.

Marni felt the coolness of the pale blue satin sheets beneath her. Paul towered over her, embraced her foot, and sucked each toe, one by one. Chills climbed up each of her vertebrates making her even more responsive to Paul's caresses. He knelt beside her, kissing the sensitive area behind her knee and then, lavishing her body with feverish kisses, his gentle, knowing hands took possession of her waiting body. She shivered as his fingers drew light circles across her nipples, then rolled them between forefinger and thumb, titillating them until her breasts swelled, aching to be devoured. He secured them in his mouth, treating them as a delicacy, savoring their essence, and she became intoxicated by the power of Paul's desire.

She felt him release her breasts and slide his body down to caress the hidden crevices of her body. Her body gyrated in response. He paused for a moment, and Marni caressed his face. His response was to meet her gaze. Her imploring eyes drew him up alongside her, and he sought her hungry lips, meshing with them instantly. They luxuriated in their exquisite ardor and then she returned the pleasure he had unselfishly given to her.

He lay quietly, but with pounding pulse, and allowed her to dominate his senses. She kissed his eyes delicately, then nibbled on his ear. She placed her mouth on his nipples and teased them until they became as taut as hers and he cried out. Then she placed her mouth around his fully extended hardness, absorbing it deep into her throat, circling it with her flicking tongue, savoring his musky taste, treasuring his moans. She brought him to the peak of arousal. Paul drew her up beside him and pressed his lips against hers. Marni wrapped her supple legs around him, and in one fluid motion he entered her.

Paul's quiet snoring disturbed Marni's slumber. She woke and found herself snuggled into the warmth of his sleeping body. Her stomach growled. She opened his right eye with her finger, looked in and said, "Hi, I'm here and I'm hungry."

Paul slid his arm under her and drew her closer. "Hello, hungry. I'm in love. Will you marry me?"

"Be serious."

"I am serious. I want to spend the rest of my life with you . . . be a family . . . have children. Why waste one precious moment apart?"

"I know we shared something spectacular tonight, but our relationship has only changed recently. There's still my divorce to get through. Have you forgotten that?"

Paul sat up and turned toward her, leaning on his elbow to meet her eyes. "Now you have a reason to speed it up. I've known you a long time. I know the kind of woman you are. Tonight, by the way you made love to me completed the part of our relationship that's been missing all these years."

"It's much too soon."

"What does time mean? Haven't we been courting for years? May be not the traditional way but it brought us here tonight." Marni smiled, knowing he was right. "You're some catch." Paul laughed. "You'll make my mother very happy." She leaned over and kissed him, sliding her arms around his neck. "I do love you," she said resting her head into his neck. "Let's talk about it over supper."

"It's right for both of us." Paul took the menu from the night table and handed it to Marni.

She skimmed it. "Surprise me," she said. She moved off the bed. "The only thing I really want. . . ."

"Is me?"

"That'll wait until after the strawberries and fresh whipped cream. How's that?"

"Delicious. And I don't mean just the strawberries and whipped cream."

"I'm going to jump into the shower." She tossed the menu onto the bed. "Your choice." She turned toward the bathroom.

The water ran down her body. Marriage, she thought. This is crazy. She told herself to calm and try to think rationally. If the truth be told she always felt something for him, more than just a business lawyer and a friend. There was no doubt about that. She just never let herself think about it seriously. She was a married woman and that meant a commitment to her husband

and their vows. The divorce released her from those restraints. Her feelings for Paul could flow freely. The love that she had for Paul sent flushes up and down her body. Her lips naturally formed a smile. The butterflies furiously fluttered in her stomach. She joined Paul in the sitting room to find the lights were dim and music was playing softly.

"May I have this dance," Paul said. They held each other and slowly moved around the sitting room. They were interrupted by room service. The table was placed in front of the windows. The flickering light of the candles reflected in the glass. Paul held out Marni's chair. He kissed her cheek. "You look beautiful."

"This is romantic," Marni said. She wondered if it would be this way after five years of marriage. As if reading her mind he said sitting down across from her, "I'm a romantic, thoroughly." She stared at him in surprise. "How did you know what I was thinking?" It was probably written all over her face.

"Doesn't that tell you something?" he said. His marriage proposal was looking better and better to Marni. "What did you order for us?" she asked.

"Beluga caviar," Paul said, as he lifted a silver cover off the chafing dish on the table, "and Fruits de Mer."

"That looks scrumptious," Marni said, "but where are my strawberries?"

"He lifted another silver cover. "Staying cold on ice." Marni placed a crepe on each of their plates and didn't waste anytime tasting it. "This is delectable."

"Do you like the selection?"

"Definitely." Marni dipped into the Beluga caviar and placed a spoonful on a piece of toast. "Heavenly."

"Did my candidness surprise you?" Paul asked. He drank some champagne. His eyes never left Marni's face.

"What do you think? It was a shock but cushioned with lots of warm thoughts I have for you. I like being married and all that goes with it. It could be wonderful with the right man."

"Are you afraid you're going to get burned again?"

"It's a consideration. I made one mistake."

"You're not the only one who lost a love?"

"That was a tragedy. The death of your wife. Mine . . . mine was growing out of a relationship. The bad part is the involvement of the children. What about them?"

"It's a package deal. I can't be their father. They have one already. I can become their friend, though, and a really good one at that." Marni had no doubt. It was for all the reasons she loved him. But a baby, she thought went along with a commitment to him. "You know my wife died pregnant with our son. I really would like a child," Paul had interrupted her thoughts. "I accept the fact that you have a career. We would share the parenting." Marni hadn't considered babies in years. She and Don were beyond that stage. Her children were in school. "And what about Greg and Neil?" she asked. "What's going to be their reaction to a new baby?" Marni really didn't want Paul to answer that. She was just thinking out loud so she half-listened to his response. "I'm sure, they'll have good and bad feelings about everything," Paul said. "That's what kids are all about," Marni said mostly to herself. Paul reached across the table for her hand. "I promise I'll be there for them." She knew he would be. He was that kind of person.

Something was bothering her so she decided to explore it. "Paul why didn't you call any of the women's numbers that I gave you?" While she waited for his answer, his lips broke into a wide grin. "How could I let my future wife fix me up?" She was flattered but a bit confused. "I knew you and Don weren't making it and that's been the case for a very long time. Hasn't it?" What could she say? She thought that she was the only one that was privy to her true feelings. "I was willing to wait," he said. "Some things Marni, darling, are worth waiting for." She felt her heart beat faster as Paul came around the table. Taking her hand in his, slowly he got down on one knee in front of her. She smiled knowing what he was about to say. "Marni will you marry me?" he asked. "I love you with all my heart and soul." Gently she embraced his face with her hands and whispered, "Yes." She drew him close to her and kissed him passionately, committing herself to him forever. This was a great moment in her life. She equated it to the birth of her sons. "I think that I want to keep our decision a secret for a while," Marni said. "I don't want anything to spoil our happiness." Paul moved away from her. She saw his loving look change to surprise and concern. "Nothing can spoil our love for each other," Paul said kissing her again. "Well, I'm afraid Don will back out of the agreement. Maybe the kids will be more upset confronted with our relationship in the midst of the divorce proceedings. I'll feel more comfortable. Just until all the papers are signed." Marni hoped that Paul would agree. When she saw the concern disappear from his face, she knew it would be all right. "If that's what you want," he said. "It'll give me an opportunity to spend time with the boys before our announcement. Let them get to know me." Marni's motherly apprehensions were dispelled by Paul's words. If she had any doubts about what she was doing, they melted away reinforcing her love for him. "You're my best friend," Marni said to Paul kissing him.

"Isn't that what marriage is?" Paul said sitting down again across from Marni again. "Best friends who happen to be great lovers, too? Can you beat that?"

"Yes," Marni said jokingly, "with strawberries and cream."

Paul laughed uncovering the dessert dish. Marni picked up a strawberry, dipped it in the whipped cream and then slowly munched on it. She looked at Paul, "Are you thinking what I'm thinking?" He grinned. "Let's go," Marni said lifting the dessert dish off the table.

Chapter Twelve

Kimberly followed Henry up the walk to his rambling shingled Cape house. "What a charming place," Kimberly said appreciating flower boxes of red geraniums beneath diamond-paned glass windows. "You're quite a gardner."

Henry shook his racquet at Kimberly in mock belligerence. "At least I'm good for something," he grumbled, not quite managing to hide a smile. "Losing two out three sets isn't a usual occurrence for me. I don't like it."

"You're lucky it's Saturday," laughed Kimberly. "During the week it would have been three straight wins." What was it about him, she wondered, that made her feel so at ease? "I can take some time and work with you on your backhand."

"Not on your life!" Henry opened the door and ushered her inside a spacious, white tiled entryway buffering an atrium abundant with plant life. "You really do have a green thumb." Kimberly couldn't believe the greenness and wealth of flowering plants. "I can't keep plants alive for very long," Kimberly admitted. "Maybe you should reconsider my offer Henry. We'll exchange expertise."

"I'll think about it but now I better get to grilling the steak. You can freshen up in the guest room," Henry said," upstairs, first door on the right."

Kimberly showered and dressed quickly, surprising herself how anxious she was to be in Henry's company. When Kimberly entered the kitchen, there were sounds of sizzling meat already cooking on the indoor barbecue grill. The hominess of Henry prepping a salad made Kimberly jealous of all the women who were fortunate enough to have this in their lives. She wondered if they knew what a valuable asset they had. She grabbed a carrot strip off the counter and sat on a bar stool. "Have you always lived here alone?"

"Only since my wife died, that's just about four years. I felt lost for a while. Now I've put together a satisfying life for myself. My time is divided amongst my practice, friends, hobbies and, of course, my children. They live here during their vacations from college, and I try to make it a home for them. I redecorated the house by myself. What do you think?"

"Very tasteful." She admired a man who took an interest in his surroundings. "It seems to suit you. I noticed your collection of African sculpture. The pieces are fascinating. Where did you get them?" She had bought similar pieces at galleries to accessorize offices and studies. "I've been traveling through Africa the last few years," Henry explained, "researching some of the herbs used by the tribal doctors." Without thinking Kimberly said, "Have you found one to rid people of evil thoughts?" Why did she say that? She was really having a good time. Kimberly noticed Henry didn't respond. "Sorry. Why spoil a good thing?" Henry touched her arm. "You're doing fine," he said. Kimberly was immediately comforted by Henry's reassurance. She wanted this date to work out.

How's Candy?"

"She seems to be doing okay. The therapy sessions with Dr. Norris seem to be working but who knows. It's only been a few weeks. She looks forward to your visits and I'm grateful for that. What do you think?"

"I think she's been honest during our conversations, but she just might be protecting herself with a fragile facade. Don't get frustrated if she regresses again. It's very possible. She's had a tough time. Where's Candy tonight?"

"She's hanging out with Nina. I didn't want to leave her alone. Since the incident, Bonita's been filling in for me, staying with Candy or driving her places. Tonight, she had a family function so Candy suggested I ask Nina and I did."

"I'm glad you're here," Henry said. "How do you like your steak?"

"Medium rare."

"Good, me too. Turn the steak while I pour our wine?"

Kimberly handled the grill while Henry lit the candles and poured the Beaujolais. "Kimberly," he said, and pulled out her chair. "Thank you," she answered sitting down. Something was happening, a feeling she never experienced before. Her eyes followed Henry's movements. He took the steak off the grill, and placed it on the carving board. "Perfect," he exclaimed as he cut the first few slices. He brought the steak along with the salad to the table. Then he sat opposite Kimberly, raised his glass with panache and said, "To happiness." She hoped it could be hers for now on. She began to eat.

"You're a beautiful dinner companion."

"That's kind of you to say, but I almost wish you had said 'interesting' dinner companion. Men always talk about my looks and forget that I have a brain.

"Let me explain," Henry said. "When I said beautiful, I meant your whole being."

"I guess I'm too sensitive. I know you're different from most men. You proved that in so many ways. I was really looking forward to seeing you tonight." There was not a moment of silence between them. She shared with him how important her career was to her and he told her how important his travels through Africa were to him. Kimberly found out they shared a mutual enjoyment of the art, music, and of course they discussed tennis. The time passed quickly. Kimberly had never spoken with a man like this before. Her conversations never went beyond her experiences at work. Sitting over coffee, Kimberly, teasingly said, "You know, Henry, I feel comfortable enough to say almost anything to you, and know you'd understand. So . . . you do the dishes. Your house, your dishes."

"Talk about sexism. What kind of role reversal is this?"

Kimberly laughed. "I'll clean off the table, you put the dishes in the dishwasher." In no time they were sitting in the living room. Kimberly found herself watching Henry pour two glasses of Baileys. To her the mundane action was the most wonderful activity in the world. Was she ridiculous?

"What are you thinking about?" Henry asked handing her a glass.

"Oh nothing."

"I can tell. You were definitely pondering some thought."

"I guess, it feels so good to be normal. Tennis. Having dinner with a friend. Henry, you made it all possible." Kimberly leaned over and kissed him on the cheek. She was surprised by her own spontaneity. "Thanks."

"Your happiness means alot to me." He put down his drink and took her drink out of her hand, drew her to him, and kissed her gently on the lips. Her body was soft, responsive to his action, but then she stiffened and moved away from him.

"What's wrong?" he asked.

"I thought it would be different with you, but it's not. I'm sorry." Kimberly picked up her drink and traced the rim of the glass with her fingers as she spoke. Her words were inaudible. "I have difficulty . . . being intimate with a man.

Henry sat back on the couch and said, "Reasonable, considering your past."

Kimberly concentrated on the circular movement of her fingers. A tear rolled down her cheek. Henry wiped it away, tenderly. "My father's sexual abuse of me really messed me up." Kimberly's eyes remained on the glass. "On my wedding night, I locked myself in the bathroom. It was George's ceaseless pleading that finally got me to open the door. Afterwards I lay on the bed staring at the ceiling, my body rigid unable to respond while George consummated the marriage. The news of my parents came after that."

Henry took Kimberly's hand. "Sex," he said softly, "is the most intimate form of communication two people can have. You must trust the other person before a relationship can be totally fulfilling. I felt you responding to me, if only for a few seconds."

"I know. Then something made me pull back." She looked at Henry and wanted him to give her words of encouragement. He did. "Don't give up, Kimberly," he said. "It'll happen when you feel comfortable enough for it to happen." Henry lightly squeezed Kimberly's hand. "I promise you." What she felt stirring inside her, she knew Henry's promise would come true. It would take time but this was what she and Dr. Norris were working toward. "Henry, I think you're right," Kimberly said as she stood. "But right now, it's getting late. I should be heading home."

"Are you sure you can drive?"

"Yes, I'm fine."

"I'll feel better if you have a cup of coffee before driving."

"Well then, just one cup," Kimberly said. "Make it black please. I really can't stay too long. Candy should be home by now."

Chapter Thirteen

"Being a babysitter is a first for me," Nina said. She was standing next to her kitchen counter mixing chocolate syrup, milk and seltzer to make Candy an egg cream. "You'll have to tell me what my responsibilities are." Nina laughed. Candy picked up the seltzer bottle and said, "Right now add some more seltzer. I like a thick foam." Nina slowly poured in more seltzer so the foam wouldn't overflow. She was glad that she had an excuse to break her date with Alan. She was tiring of him. He would soon become a collector's item joining the others on her wall. "How's that?" Nina asked handing the glass to Candy. Candy guzzled down half the egg cream. "Really good," she said. "You're the best babysitter. If I couldn't stay here tonight, Mom wouldn't keep her date with Henry. I wanted her to go. He's a good guy." Nina waved her hand in the air. "Ask me anytime. You have an open invitation." She started to put together two more glasses of egg creams. "Hey . . . look over the trees!" Nina said. "It's a full moon." Candy leaning over the sink, put her empty glass in the basin and then looked out the window. "Oh, I see it," Candy said. "A full moon is spooky," Nina bellowed. "All the crazy people come out tonight." Nina dangled her fingers in Candy's face and squeaked, "Ha, ha, ha, I'm going to get you." Nina let Candy brush her fingers aside and she immediately finished the egg creams. "You're kooky," Candy said. "Rule Number One, a babysitter never tries to scare the kid or else there'll be nightmares." Nina hoped she wasn't serious. "Sorry about that," Nina said flippantly. Candy took the glass off the counter and added more seltzer. "Rule Number Two," Nina said, "next time, you make your own egg cream. My father taught me and I'll teach you the family secret." Nina tasted her handiwork. "The best. It's my favorite drink. When you finish yours Candy, I'll show you around."

"Can we go now? I promise I won't spill my drink."

"Okay, I'm a pushover as a babysitter," Nina said. "But don't think you can walk all over me. I draw the line sometimes. Right now, follow me," she said. The kitchen space flowed into the dining room and living room. "It seems like I'm living in a loft," Nina said walking through the area. "I love it. The picture windows not only make it bright and airy in here but brings the feeling of mother nature inside. That's the artist in me talking."

"Aren't you afraid the windows will break in a storm?"

"Don't even think about it."

Nina opened a door near the staircase. "If you ever want to sleep over, I have a guest room. It has its own bath." Candy looked around. "Thanks for the invite."

They walked up the staircase. It was metal, painted black with rectangular floating steps. A curved pipe railing was made to look as if it was suspended in space but it was a connection to the upper levels. They stopped on the second landing where there were two master bedroom suites with lavish bathrooms done up in white marble. "I guess the former occupants believed in separate but equal quarters," Nina said as she and Candy paraded through them.

"It does seem odd," Candy said. She followed Nina to the top of the staircase. "Boy, I hate to climb this in the dark. You miss a step and you're dead." Nina never thought of such a thing. She was going up to her ivory tower. "Oh, you get use to it." She flipped on the lights in her studio.

"What a studio," Candy said glancing around. "Wow with all this glass you can count the stars. It's so neat. You need a telescope to pick out the constellations."

"That's an idea," Nina said. "I'm going to buy one."

Candy walked around, picking up paint brushes, pads filled with sketches and canvases resting against the walls. Finally she stopped in front of Nina's gallery of men. "You're into abstracts. How come you have all these paintings?" Candy asked.

"Well . . . how should I put it," Nina said. "Let me think for a minute. It's my acting out wall," Nina finally answered.

"I get it. I guess, you can say I acted out in the guest house." Candy looked at the half-finished egg cream for a second. "I don't have a father like yours," she said to Nina. "My father is an alcoholic. One night he was drinking so much that he raped me thinking I was Mom. We look so much alike, blond hair, green eyes, five feet seven inches, and my nose even turns up like hers." Nina was shocked by what she heard. It was so far from what Pops meant to her. "Poor kid," Nina groaned. "There's a reason you're screwed up." Nina hearing her own words felt she had stepped over her boundaries of good manners. "I'm sorry," she said, "I shouldn't have been so blunt."

"It doesn't matter," Candy said, "how you say it. It's the truth. I try to be a good person, and do what's expected of me, but sometimes I get so damn confused. It's impossible for me to manage my actions. Dr. Norris says at these times I display impetuous behavior."

"I understand Candy but it's important to learn self-control. Your mother is concerned." Nina now knew what Kimberly was never able to tell Marni and herself. "Don't turn her off. You need each other." She remembered her own mother's love and what it meant to her. "Mom and I have been really good lately," Candy said. Nina gave Candy's arm a love pat. That's what I like to hear," she said.

"I already told you I was a wild one," Nina said standing beside Candy. She glanced up and down the wall of portraits. "Living on the edge. High on life itself. Believing, everything will eventually be perfect for me. Take a good look at the wall in front of you, that's what I've got to show for it. Thank god for my success as an artist. It's the reason I wake up each day. Think about your actions. Listen to what I'm saying." Nina couldn't believe she was giving advice. It blew her mind but she sort of liked the role. "I'll try, that's what I said to Dr. Norris and Mommy." Nina gave Candy a quick embrace. "You're a good kid," she said. "Things will work out for you."

"I hope so. Although you're old, I feel that I can talk to you." Nina didn't know if she should thank Candy for the compliment or be upset because of the age factor. "My door is always open," Nina said graciously. "I'll even throw in some art lessons, if you're interested."

"Thanks. I'll think about it. I get good marks in art class."

Candy slowly walked alongside the wall. She stopped in front of Marty's portrait. After a few seconds she said to Nina, "Do you think you could introduce me to him? He looks very hot in those tight shorts." What would Marty want with Candy, Nina thought, when he could have an experienced lover, screw the age factor. "You're a pisser," Nina said cherishing Candy's honesty. She wasn't about to disillusion her young friend. They laughed walking down the staircase.

Candy glanced at her watch. "I better go now. Mom said she'll be back by elevenish. Thanks for a great evening." Candy slipped into her jacket. "I enjoyed it," Nina said placing a kiss on Candy's cheek. "Think about the lessons."

Candy sat contentedly on the living room couch, snacking on milk and cookies while watching "Saturday Night Live." She waited for her mother to return from her date with Henry. A buzzing sound caused Candy to jump up, ending her sedentary position. She spilled the plate of cookies from her lap onto the floor. Realizing it was the intercom connected to the gate, she pressed the button to speak. "Who's there?" she called.

"It's your father, honey," the voice responded from the other end.

"What are you doing here?" she asked. "What do you want?"

"I want to talk to you, baby," George said. "Open the gate."

"You're not supposed to be here. Please go away."

"I want to see you."

"Mother will be very angry if I let you in. Have you been drinking?"

"I'm cold sober, Candy."

"I don't want to see you. Go away."

"Please Candy, it'll be all right, baby. I promise. Just like it was the last time, when I met you after school."

"I don't know."

"I'm your father. I love you."

"Okay, but just for a little while."

She buzzed the gate open and picked up the cookies until she heard his knock. Letting him in she remained near the foyer entrance to the living room. He sat where she was seated earlier. Then Candy moved to the club chair across from him. His once good looks had been swallowed by the puffiness of alcohol abuse. His face marred with red splotches and his blue eyes enclosed with crusty lines.

"It's so good to see you, Candy," George said. His right eye was twitching. "I've missed you so much—and your mother too." He pointed to the cushion next to him. "Come, sit over here so we can talk."

Candy sat on the arm of the club chair across from her father.

"I did something terrible," George said running his fingers through his blond hair. "I know that and I've been in therapy ever since. I'm very sorry. It wasn't my intention to hurt you, but I already told you all of this, honey. Now I really want my family back." His voice cracked. It took me all day to work up courage to come here tonight. It means alot to me."

"What can I say?" Candy said. Her head was bent. Her eyes were focused on the fringe of the oriental rug. Finally she said, "We had fun when we went boating. My rides in the golf cart with you were special. They were the good times we had together. But I also remember when you ignored me. I wanted your love so much. It wasn't until I learned about substance abuse in school did I find out the truth about you. Mom always made excuses for you."

"Honey, I'm over all that. I always loved you, but sometimes it was difficult for me to show you. Let me make it up to you."

"I think it's too late for that. I'm learning that it's not healthy for me to be with you. When I see you, I get mixed up and do terrible things."

George got up and walked toward Candy. He wanted to console his daughter. The door banged open and Kimberly flew into the room. She had recognized George's license plate. "Don't you dare touch her," she screamed. "Get away from her." She turned to Candy. "How could you have let him in?"

"Kimberly, you have every right to be angry," George said, his voice calm, his eyes never leaving Kimberly's face. "But please, listen to me. Candy and I were having a friendly father and daughter conversation, that's all.

"Father," Kimberly raged. "You call yourself a father even after you rape her. How could you?"

"That was an accident. You must know that."

"Does it matter, George? You did it."

"I was drunk. I didn't do it on purpose. She's my daughter. I love her." George's hands were shaking.

"You don't know how to love," Kimberly's mind was only filled with angry thoughts. "You're a sick person who has messed up all our lives." Her chest tightened making it difficult for her breathe. She stopped shouting long enough to take a deep breath. "I'm cursed with you for the rest of my life, just like my father said."

"Kimberly, it has nothing to do with your father. I had too much to drink, that's all. I made a mistake. Please, I want my family back."

"I'll see you dead first." Angrily, she picked up the intercom. "Alex, this is Mrs. Mathews. Please come to my apartment in your car. Thank you." Kimberly looked at George, tears ran down his face. "Get in your car," she said to him, "and don't ever come back. Alex will escort you off the grounds."

"Won't you ever forgive me, Kimberly?" It was incredible to hear these words coming out of George's mouth. "Forgive you!" Kimberly shrieked. "Never. I can't forgive myself for not leaving you sooner. That's what I should have done to protect Candy." George cried but he was unable to sway Kimberly's mind. "I didn't mean to hurt her," he wept. "I didn't mean to hurt you either. I love you both," he sobbed. "Please let us talk it out. Dr. Freemont thinks we should all go to counseling together. Kimberly, let's do it for Candy's sake." Kimberly looked at Candy for a second. What George was saying made sense. But she couldn't sit with him in the same room. She couldn't behave rationally. She was beyond that. Similarly, if her father was alive she couldn't go to church with him. "Just stay away from Candy and everything will be fine," Kimberly said. "If you love us, you'll do that. Do you understand, George?" There was a knock on the door. Kimberly let Alex in. "Please escort Mr. Mathews to the gate," she said.

Candy stared at Alex.

"Yes, Ma'am," Alex said. "This way, sir."

George glared at Kimberly. "I'll leave now, but she's my daughter too. I'll be back."

Kimberly stood near her open door and watched the cars go

down the driveway. She sighed. "How long do I have until the next time?" She shivered in the cold night realizing she actually deceived herself by hoping she could sustain some happiness in her life. Several minutes later Alex returned he told her that George had left the grounds. Kimberly went inside. Slowly, she walked to the couch and rested her body against the soft cushions. A voice inside her kept chanting; you're no better than your mother, you're no better than your mother. Solitude enveloped her; Kimberly closed her eyes. Exhausted, she fell asleep for a few moments. Something woke her up. Her instincts told her to check on Candy. She hadn't seen her since George left the house.

Laboriously, Kimberly ascended the staircase and stood before her daughter's closed bedroom door. She knocked. "Candy? Candy, are you sleeping, honey?" There was no response. She knocked again, more loudly, and tried the doorknob. It was locked. "Candy, answer me," she yelled. There was still nothing. She ran downstairs and called Alex. Within minutes Kimberly and Alex were running up the stairs. Kimberly again pounded on the door, turning the knob vigorously, but there still was no response. Alex pushed her aside and lunged at the door with his shoulder forcing it open. Candy was sprawled across the bed, face-down, motionless, an empty bottle on the floor beside her. Kimberly ran to her and shook her hard. Candy stirred.

Alex picked up the bottle. "Oh, shit," he said.

"Candy," Kimberly cried, "why did you let him in?" Kimberly stood helpless as Alex flopped Candy over. "What should I do?" she asked. "Should I call the police?"

"No. Not the police," Alex snapped. "Call an ambulance."

Alex supported Candy in a sitting position. He knelt before her, holding her hands so she wouldn't fall back. Then he put both her hands in one of his, and with his free hand he lightly slapped her face. "You idiot," he shouted. "Open your eyes. Come on, come on." Candy opened them but only for a split second. "Come on, Candy! I'll help you walk. Don't go to sleep." He dragged her across the room a few times, then stopped at the bathroom where he forced her to vomit.

"What are you doing?" Kimberly cried.

"Trying to save her life," Alex yelled. When Candy finished, Alex flushed and took a towel from next to the sink. He wet it with cool water and washed Candy's face. "That should make you feel better," he said reassuringly, all the while he supported her with one hand. Candy's eyes opened but were dazed. Her body was limp as a stuffed doll. "She'll be all right," Alex told Kimberly. "Help me walk her. We can't let her sleep."

As Candy was marched around the room, she moaned, "Please leave me alone . . . let me sleep."

"Just keep walking," Alex demanded.

When the ambulance arrived, Marni ran out of the house, wrapped in a robe. "I heard the siren," she said. "What happened?" Kimberly grabbed Marni's arm. "It's Candy," she said, "she took some pills. We're going to the hospital, Nassau Medical." Then Kimberly followed Candy into the back of the vehicle. "I'll throw on some clothes," Marni said, "and meet you there." The ambulance doors were closed before Kimberly responded.

"She'll be fine, Mrs. Mathews," the resident said. "We've pumped her stomach and there should be no physical side affects. She's really quite lucky, whoever helped her earlier this evening saved her life."

"Yes," Kimberly said, "we were lucky to have Alex."

"You have a beautiful daughter," the resident said in the waiting room. "It's a shame that something like this had to happen, but to be honest, I see it all the time."

"When we get Candy home, I'll make sure this never happens again," Kimberly said. "It shouldn't have happened this time."

How could she make sure it doesn't happen? Could she be with Candy every minute of her waking hours? Why couldn't he just leave them alone?

"She can't be released without a psychological examination," the resident said. "That's the law."

"She's under the care of a therapist," Kimberly said. "I'll call her." Dr. Norris and Henry told her it wasn't going to be easy.

"Is she associated with the hospital?" the doctor asked.

"I don't know," Kimberly said but she surely wasn't going to start with someone new. She depended on Dr. Norris. "Don't worry, I'll take care of the matter."

"Henry is," Marni said knowing that Kimberly was seeing him. "You can always call him."

"First I'll try Dr. Norris." She would call her early in the morning. Kimberly took a deep breath and said to Marni, "It was George. He came over tonight to see Candy after she left Nina's place. That's why she tried to kill herself. As if he hasn't done enough to her already."

"What are you talking about?" Marni asked.

"Marni," Kimberly cried out, "I hate him so much."

Chapter Fourteen

Marni opened the apartment door. Don stood there wiping his palms on his trousers. "Hello, Don," she said, "I'm glad you finally made it. You do remember that both of us are parents, don't you?"

"Oh, Marni," Don said, "it's just been a little rough lately. I've had terrible problems. People are not buying cars, and Barbara has been sick."

"Anything serious?" she said thinking did she really care. She knew Don, if he were here, he had something important to tell her. "Depends on how you look at it," he said. "Well come in and sit down," she said pointing to the sofa. Marni noticed Don couldn't look her in the eye. "What's the matter Don? Tell me." She waited a few minutes then Don said, "Barbara is pregnant." Marni was taken by surprise with what she had just heard. "We still have to work out the children's support agreement." Her mind became cluttered with things she wanted to say. She paced the living room floor to help her think.

"I was upset when we found out," Don explained. "I couldn't believe the stupid rabbit died.

Marni stopped pacing to look at him. There was no longer a loving veil to soften the effects of time. His once full head of sandy hair was receding and speckled with gray. The twinkling blue eyes that first attracted her to him were tired and distant. His athletic body now was slumping into the cushions. "How's Barbara taking it?"

"She was hysterical. She realized the complications it could bring to our relationship. I told her when we first started seeing each other I had no interest in more children. But, since she doesn't have children and we were planning to get married anyway, I told her that I would respect her decision. What could I say? If she wanted to go through with the pregnancy, it would be fine with me. If she wanted to end the pregnancy, it was up to her. She had my support whatever her decision. Afterall, I had to take responsibility for my actions."

"That's very mature," Marni said. His speech sounded so rehearsed to her. Something he read in a manual for the modern man. "She's glad that she's pregnant now, except for the nausea," he said. "I'm feeling good about having a baby and settling down." Marni wandered how she could have married Don. What was she thinking? Did she change so much from their wedding day? "I guess, you were running a marathon for sixteen years. Never crossing the final line. What a way to be married!" Marni bemoaned.

"Come on, give me a break, Marni."

"Oh, what's the use," she said shaking her head. Why waste her words? It's over. Now let this work for Greg and Neil. "Anything else that you want to tell me?" Marni waited impatiently. She wanted to hear what he had to say and then take the necessary steps to move the divorce along. "I'm keeping the house," Don mumbled. "But I'll make it up to you in the agreement." Marni plopped down in the armchair. "Oh, you mean eventually we're going to finish the divorce." She thought that was good news. "I'll refinance the mortgage on the house and with that money buy out your share." Marni thought for a second. "That's changing our agreement," she said. "We were selling the house and splitting the profit." She really didn't care what happened to the house. Her concern would be to make sure that she received her share of the money. However, she now saw a way to get Don to agree to the child support. "It shouldn't matter to you," he said. "You were never moving back to the house." Marni shrugged her shoulders. "It matters," she said. "I don't think it's a good idea keeping the house. The boys are going to be upset, jealous of a new baby living in their house." Don moved to the edge of the cushion. "It was your choice to move out. They'll have to understand." Marni shook her head. "Why not show some responsibility toward the kids you already have. How about agreeing to equally share the child support with me?"

"Why does everything have to be your way, Marni?"

"This isn't my way, Don. This is what's right."

"Money's tight," he groaned. "I'm starting a new family."

"Does that mean you forget the children that you have already?" She heard no answer from him. She caught him in a situation that he'd better step up to the batter's plate and become a real father. "I won't sign over the deed unless you agree to my terms. It's for your children's welfare. I mean what I'm saying. Don't start decorating until you speak to your attorney."

"I'm not decorating or anything. I told you, money will be tight for a while. But you are managing very well," Don declared looking around. "The child support must be adequate."

"The nominal amount was only temporary until we worked out an agreement. I've been keeping a record of all my expenditures so that we can make the necessary adjustment."

"Stop pressuring me, Marni."

"I didn't put you in this predicament. You did a fine job all by yourself. Have you really thought about a new family? The responsibilities? The consequences? I think you and Barbara should reconsider."

"Stop telling me what to do," Don shouted. "I don't belong to you anymore. Why can't you just wish me well?"

"Because I think you're being despicable to our children. Speaking about our children, you're going to tell them about the baby. Right?"

"Baby, whose baby?" Greg asked as he and Neil walked in.

Don blanched as his sons leaned down to kiss him hello. Taking hold of each of their hands, he said, "I have something to tell you." Don swallowed hard. "Barbara is going to have a baby."

Greg pulled his hand away. "I knew this was going to happen. Now you're going to forget us. Like we don't exist."

"Don't be so stupid, Greg," Don responded.

"Sure, sure," Greg shouted.

"I admit, it'll be difficult at first, as it always is, when there is a new baby around, but I'll do my best to see you."

"Just like the past four weeks, huh, Dad."

"Actions speak louder than words," Marni said. "Don, you know what you have to do."

"Dr. Gordon says it's quality time that counts."

"That's if you show up," Greg said.

"Greg has a very good point," Marni said. It was important to support her son. He must be feeling abandoned by his father.

"I'm sorry I didn't make time. Barbara wasn't feeling well and we were busy making arrangements for her to move into our house."

"I suppose the baby gets my room."

"Well . . . you and Neil can still have your rooms when you sleep over. The guest bedroom will become the nursery. How's that?"

"Maybe you should check with Barbara," Greg said, "before you say anything."

"Don't be disrespectful. I'm your father."

"Yeah . . . sure."

"Is Barbara going to be with us every time we see you?" Neil asked. Don turned toward him. "I don't want to spend time with her. I just want to be with you."

"We'll see," Don said. "It'll be her house too. We'll have to try to work things out."

"I think it's important that the boys get to spend time with just you," Marni said.

"I'll do my best, Marni."

"It's the pits," Neil said.

"It'll be okay," Don said. "You'll see. We'll have plenty of time, just for us. Barbara is just like Mom. She hates sports on television."

Marni wondered how else they were alike. Seeing what happened between Don and the kids, she felt sorry for them. They weren't asked to be born and now all they wanted was a father who cared.

"Fellas," Don said, "let's have dinner together."

"I don't want to," Greg said. "I lost my appetite."

"Come on, Greg," Don pleaded. "I haven't seen you for a long time."

"Whose fault was that?"

"I'll take you to your favorite restaurant," Don pleaded. "Cut me some slack."

"Let's go," Neil said, urging his brother.

"Go on, Greg," Marni said. "Talk to your father over dinner." If Don was making the effort to take them out to dinner, Greg should go. Marni assumed her usual role of director when it came to Don and the children. It was right she did it, afterall she had her sons' best interests at heart. She was always the adult in her relationship with Don. Her role hadn't changed even with the pending divorce. When Marni saw Greg shrug his shoulders she knew that he decided to go with this father. Wanting to reinforce his decision positively she said, "That's very understanding and mature of you." Greg looked at her and without any words from him Marni just knew that they were on the same wave length.

When Marni closed the door behind them, she thought about Paul and if they had a child. "What a mess," she muttered. Then she told herself Paul wasn't Don. Somehow they would work through this extended family situation. She had no doubts about that. Tomorrow, early in the morning she would call Steven Butler and ask for a hearing. Marni felt that in the light of the development, she had to fight harder for her children's rights. But now there was room for negotiation.

Chapter Fifteen

Nina stood by the kitchen counter pouring just a little of Pouilly Fuisse in a chilled wine goblet. She tasted the wine swirling it around in her mouth to get its true essence before swallowing it. It was perfect.

The intercom buzzer went off just as she walked into the living room carrying a tray with the wine and two goblets. She was expecting Alan. Hearing his voice through the speaker, she opened the gate. Soon after, she swung her front door open. Standing before her, Alan had tucked under one arm a package, gift wrapped in blue paper, and hanging on the other arm was a tall blonde good-looking woman. Nina immediately labeled her a hot dish because of her clothing. She was skimpily dressed in a tank top and short skirt with a motorcycle jacket thrown over her shoulders. Alan introduced her as his business associate, Veronica.

Nina wondered what Alan had planned as she led them toward a pale green leathery sectional centered in the living room. Stepping aside, Nina gave them access to the horseshoe seating. "Make yourself at home," Nina said taking a closer look at Veronica. "Alan has told me so much about you," Veronica said sitting down. She ran her hand over the soft leather. "Mmm," she muttered. "Expensive stuff." Nina was amused. "Thanks," Nina said. "I had to sell many paintings to afford it."

Veronica placed a cigar in her mouth and Alan quickly lit it and one for himself. Then he seated himself next to her. The smell of tobacco permeated the room. Nina couldn't stand the odor. "Do you mind putting out those things?" Nina said. Her eyes followed spirals of smoke ascending to the ceiling. "Don't you people know smoking can kill you?" An expression of condescension was shared by Alan and Veronica. "So we'll die happy," Veronica said. Nina was really annoyed. First they light up without asking her permission and now they're obnoxious enough not to put the cigars out. "I mean it, stop puffing and give me those things. I'm going to throw them out in the kitchen. I hate the smell of a cigar."

"Cigar smoking is the new rage but have it your way," Alan said taking the cigar out of Veronica's mouth and then handing both of them to Nina. Nina was relieved. "What's your position in Alan's firm?" Nina asked Veronica on her way to the kitchen. "I'm the gal Friday," Veronica proudly stated pushing her chest forward. "And Saturday and Sunday, too," Nina said sarcastically. She was annoyed Alan brought someone to her home without checking with her first. "Actually, I'm on duty twenty-four hours, Nina. The hours are long, but I love my job. Everyone makes me feel so important." I bet, Nina thought. Nina returned from the kitchen spraying potpourri and holding another goblet. "I hope, Alan is compensating you adequately, time and a half for after hours." She sat across from Alan and Veronica and filled all three goblets. "Are you Alan?" Nina asked facetiously. "It's none of your business but I'll tell you anyway, she's compensated very well. Veronica is worth every penny." Alan leaned over to pat Veronica's knees. "No job is too small or too large for her, and she's so willing; that's very important to me." Nina lifted her goblet to salute Veronica. "Let me see," she said. "Would you call her a business asset or a business expense?" Nina laughed. "Don"t be a bitch," Alan said. "Everyone has a right to work," Nina replied. "I apologize Veronica. Just make sure you agree with your . . . usage." Alan quickly retorted, "Her treatment is her problem, not yours. No more discussion." Nina shook her finger in Alan's direction. "Very touchy," she said. "Womens' rights are important to me."

"Let's drop that topic," Alan said. "I'm anxious to see my finished portrait. When is the unveiling?"

"Right now." Nina stood and led them toward the stairway leading to her studio. Alan allowed the women to go ahead of him. They each carried a wine glass and Alan brought along the mystery gift.

Looking at the package Nina said to Alan, "What do you have there?"

"It's a present for all of us. You'll see it later."

Nina walked over to a covered canvas propped up on a table and with a dramatic sweeping gesture, she flipped off the sheet. It was a painting of a nude man closely resembling Alan, standing sidewise looking out the window so that his erection was clearly visible. Veronica's eyes nearly popped out of her head. "Wow," she exclaimed loudly.

"This isn't what I posed for," Alan said. "This is beyond an artist's license."

Nina laughed. "You're a schmuck, Alan, and sometimes a very big one." She noticed the hurt look on Alan's face.

Veronica moved closer to the painting and using her finger, pointed to a brown mark. "This could be you, Alan," she said pointing to the tip of the penis. "You've got a freckle right there sweetie."

Alan's face reddened. "I don't think this is very humorous."

"Oh, Alan, it was just a joke," Nina said. She directed them to another canvas resting on an easel facing the window. Nina turned the easel around and placed it right under the track light. The painting was of Alan partially clothed in a white toga, revealing an evenly tanned body, dwarfing a replica of the coliseum in the background.

"It's fabulous," Veronica said to Nina. "You really are an artist."

"Well, thank you, dear," Nina said.

Alan smiled proudly. "I had no idea how it would turn out. It's so strong." He looked toward Nina's gallery of men.

"I bet I know what you're thinking," Nina said looking at her other portraits. "Mine is the best." Alan kissed her on the lips and then handed her the gift box. Nina started opening the gift as she dropped to the floor and sat on an air mattress. She loved opening presents. Ripping off the last bit of paper she exclaimed, "Body Paints."

"Yes," Alan said, "tonight is my turn to be the artist. I want to give you and Veronica the thrill of my talent."

"Both of us?" Nina asked.

Veronica had already begun to take off her clothing.

Nina got up and walked to the door. "Why don't you two begin? I'll bring up the wine bottle." She needed to think about her participation. Something was eating at her gut. She walked back into the studio a few minutes later. She stood at the door watching Alan use metallic green paint to meticulously fill an outline of a serpent. He had drawn it slithering down Veronica's beautiful prone body. Alan started his painting at her right breast, moved diagonally across her stomach, and ended with an open-fanged mouth positioned to attack her most private parts. "That's grotesque, Alan but very well done."

"Don't just stand there watching," Alan said. "Join us."

"I don't think so. Tonight I'm . . . the voyeur."

"Oh, come on. I thought, you'd get a kick out this. Since when are you a wallflower?"

Looking at Veronica all painted up, Nina's adventuresome spirit was sparked. "Oh, what the hell," she said. She hadn't done anything like this for a long time. Nina gulped down the wine. She took off her clothes and knelt down on the mattress beside them. A menage a trois wasn't new to her. She preferred two men and herself, but this was Alan's fantasy, as he had initiated it, and Veronica was a sexually enticing woman, wetting her appetite.

Nina waiting her turn, anticipated the titillating sensation with each of Alan's brush strokes. Alan leaned over and kissed Veronica's nipples. "You're beautiful," he said to her, then turned to Nina. Goose bumps erupted on Nina's skin as Alan began to paint. He encircled both breasts with oversized, bright red lips, out of which emerged an exaggerated tongue descending from her cleavage and inching toward her mass of soft black curls. His imagination was stimulated by her immediate response to his every stroke.

"Nina love," Veronica said, flushed with excitement, "you're magnificent." Veronica leaned over and gently caressed Nina's shoulder as Alan finished. Nina, her raw sexuality already aroused, responded in kind, touching Veronica in ways and in places that would bring them both to the heights of sensual awareness. Then she extended her reach and fondled Alan. They formed a multi-limbed animal, writhing on the mattress, shrieking with sounds of pleasure. Suddenly Nina disentangled herself. "Out," she shouted to Alan and Veronica. "Get out."

Alan sat up and leaned on his arm. "Why?" he said. "Just get out," she shouted in his face. She was relieved when she saw Alan and Veronica stand. She did the same. "I'm disappointed," he said putting his legs into his trousers. "So am I," Nina exclaimed looking at her body.

After Alan and Veronica left, Nina washed off the bizarre body painting and compulsively straightened up her studio. She added Alan's portrait to her gallery. Studying it for a moment, she asked herself why she had draped most of Alan's manhood, leaving the barest tip exposed. It could be missed if you didn't linger. Nina wanted the meaningless game with men to be over. She thought that she was committed to follow her belief until uncertainty chipped away some of her strength.

Walking past the other portraits, again she became more convinced that using men for her pleasures was over for her. She stopped in front of Pierre. It was still a habit of hers whenever she needed to talk. "That's it, Pierre," she said. She spoke quietly but resolutely. "I've had enough of this shit. I want the fusing of feelings that I had with you. Yes, I still remember them and sometimes even feel them. No more escapes for the moment just to satisfy lust. It leaves me cold and empty. Another has been added to the collection, but I swear he's the last. Contentment will come from my painting, at least until I can find someone who can replace you in my heart." She left her studio knowing in the morning she would return and be ready to make her paintbrush mean something again.

Chapter Sixteen

Marni watched Greg and Neil show off to Paul their ice skating skill. It was Paul's idea to spend time with the boys doing something they enjoyed. Marni arranged a Sunday outing to the ice skating rink. "Hey, Paul," Neil shouted, "Watch." With both toes perfectly angled with the ice, Neil spun around in a complete circle. "Paul, watch me," Greg said. First he built up speed skating right by Neil. Then he extended one leg balancing himself perfectly, and twirled. Paul, gripping the railing of the rink, had been looking across the ice to the area set aside for figure skaters and watched the performance. Zealously he clapped his hands above his head acknowledging their feats. His enthusiastic praise caused Paul to lose his balance and grab Marni for support. "Don't let go," he shouted, "my derriere doesn't need another crack. It's my head that must be cracked. Whose idea was this anyway?" Marni pressed her index finger into Paul's chest. Then she said, "Yours, remember." She hoped the day worked out. She steadied Paul against herself and watched Greg and Neil racing around, bouncing to the rhythms of the disco music blasting through the speakers above the rink. Red, green and blue lights flashed to the music. "It must be a long time since you've skated," Marni said. "That's an accurate statement," Paul said and laughed. "Not since I was kid. I'm having a great time, though." She hoped so. Marni tried to spend at least some part of each weekend with the kids. Remembering these family outings she resented Don the most. His reluctance to join them and her need to drag him out of the door put a damper on any enjoyment realized. Don preferred to stay home and watch sports on television. Seeing Paul today with the kids, she knew that he meant what he said. Marriage was a package deal.

"I thought real estate brokers worked on the weekends?" Paul said.

"Only in the morning if I have to. I try to just work on Saturday. The kids like to be with their friends, then." She wondered how the schedule would change if Don wanted to see them every Sunday.

"I know you were worried about today," Paul said, "but the kids and I are just fine." Marni caught a glimpse of her sons weaving in and out among other skaters. "At least, so far," Marni said. She wandered if he sensed that she was uptight. Kids were super sensitive, especially in this situation. "If there's a problem," Paul assured her, "I'll work it out." She had confidence in Paul's ability relating to the kids. The concern was that Paul was Mommy's boyfriend. It was a big deal in her sons' mind, especially since Mommy never had one before. The security blanket had a wrinkle. There would be some shared time. She was a realist. There would be tough going. "Watch out," Marni shouted, "here come the kids." Greg and Neil locked arms with Marni and Paul. They skated four abreast, whipping around the rink, barely missing the other skaters. Marni glanced at the three smiling faces and got a kick out of the scene.

"Hey! Slow down," Paul shouted. "Have some respect for age." The kids laughed and pulled faster. Finally Marni yelled, "Stop, I need a break." The boys dropped them at the rink exit. Winded, she and Paul walked off the ice. Marni rubbed her aching angles thinking she could just about imagine what Paul was feeling but he stood stoically next to her revealing no aches or pains. After two hours, the long-awaited announcement came over the speaker. "Take your last turn around the rink, five minutes until the session is over. Thanks for coming. Hope we see you soon."

"Marni, shall we take our last spin?" Paul asked, slipping his arm around her. She looked down at his ankles and was surprised to see they weren't turning in. "Are you sure you want to do this?" He answered without a seconds hesitation, "I'm fine." Gliding smoothly around the rink, Marni noticed a marked improvement in his skill. "You're right Paul, you're doing fine." He laughingly said, "The Catch is a born athlete." Marni laughed too.

When all four were taking off their skates, Marni announced to Greg and Neil, "Paul would like to take us for some pizza.

Okay?" Greg gave Neil the thumbs up sign. "Let's go to Vinny's," Greg said. "They have the best pizza." Paul looked first at Marni and then Neil, "Any objections?" Marni knew Neil wouldn't say anything. She always took the kids there. Shortly thereafter, they piled into Paul's car.

"That was so much fun, Paul," Greg said. "Thanks." Marni liked what she just heard. She was feeling good about the day. The spirited group was sitting at a round table in Vinny's, waiting for their Cokes and pizza. "You know," Greg teased, "I couldn't believe how funny you looked on skates." Marni banged Greg's elbow and said, "Hey, Paul was doing great at the end."

"That's right," Paul said.

"Well, I guess so," Greg said. "We use to force my father to skate with us. He was afraid to hurt his ankles then he couldn't play tennis."

"Do you play tennis?" asked Paul.

"Yes. Sometimes Neil and I play against Dad," Greg answered.

"Who wins?"

"Dad. He's really a good player," Greg said. "Do you play tennis?"

"Sure, I like all sports."

"I do too, but I like soccer the best," Greg said. The server brought their drinks. Neil took his straw and blew the paper into Paul's face.

"Neil," Marni said, "that's not necessary." Then she caught a glimpse of what Paul was doing and wasn't happy. She wondered if she should say anything. Everything was going so well. Paul nonchalantly took the wrapper off his straw and tore a piece off the end. In his mouth he rolled the paper into a wet ball. Then he placed it in the straw and blew. Whomp . . . Paul hit Neil. Marni knew this was going to get out of hand. She had been witness to this kind of fun often.

Whomp . . . Neil hit Greg.

"Neil," Marni said. "We're not the only ones in the restaurant." Marni knew when Neil closed his ears to what she was saying. The table became a battlefield. Heads bent preparing the ammunition. Lips mounted around extended straws. Eyes sighted targets. Little wet balls crisscrossed in the air. Victims lightly rubbed the landing spot. Whomp . . . Marni finally decided to join in. She wanted to be part of the group but she hit the server. "Oh, I'm so sorry," Marni said apologetically. The server quickly put down the pizza and left. Marni joined the others laughing, both at themselves and at Neil, who mimicked the ladies's surprised expression.

Back at Marni's apartment, Marni and Greg were spectators to Paul and Neil playing intendo.

"Who else is thirsty besides me?" Marni asked.

"I am, Mom," Greg said.

"Me too," Neil said.

"Count me in," Paul said, sitting on the den floor with his eyes tracking the action on the television screen. "You won again Neil, but it was a close game."

"My turn," Greg said.

"Four teas coming up," Marni said going into the kitchen. She thought Paul was doing a good job of managing the situation.

"As a first timer," Greg said to Paul, "you did all right. But I'm going to beat your brains in." Greg took his position next to Paul on the floor. "We'll see," Paul answered. "Set up the game, Greg."

"Hey," Greg said, moving his stick, "do you like my mother?"

"Sure do. She's terrific."

"My parents' divorce is the worst thing that could have happened to me."

"I can understand that."

"And now my Dad and his girlfriend are going to a have baby. I haven't seen him much since they're living together. I doubt we'll see him at all after this baby comes." "Have you spoken to him about this," Paul asked.

"Yeah. So what. What does that mean?"

"Don't give up on him." Paul touched Greg's shoulder.

"Are you thinking of marrying my Mom?" Paul didn't hesitate to answer Greg. "I really like her a lot. Let's see what happens."

"Mom gets married to you, maybe you have kids. Where does that leave Neil and me?"

"Let's just say, if we do get married and have children it means you're the older brother, just like Neil's older brother. The love and family support will always be there. I'm not your father but I can have a place in your life. Your mother and I were friends for a very long time. I've been your mother's lawyer since she opened her office. She's told me so many great things about you and Neil. I'm really looking forward to our friendship. How about it?" Paul tried to shake Greg's hand but Greg kept both hands on the stick maneuvering the little people on the screen. Greg finally said, "I guess." Paul turned to Neil. "You've been very quiet through this. So?"

"This kid in my class . . . his parents are getting a divorce," Neil said. "He told me my mother would find a boyfriend. I guess, you're it."

"I heard that," Marni said standing with the tray.

"Are you going to marry him?" Neil asked his mother.

Marni put down the tray. She always believed her relationship with her sons should be based on honesty. "What do you think about that?" She really wanted to ease the kids into her new relationship with Paul. "First Dad," Greg said. "Now you. I feel like a displaced person." Marni walked over to Greg and sat on the floor next to him. "I'll never desert you. You're my oldest son forever. You can't get rid of me even if you try." She turned to Neil. "Come over here," she said taking both her sons' hands. "This has been a rough time in your life. I'm sorry it ever happened but it did. I can't change it. I love you both very much and I'll do everything in my power to be there for both of you. Your father and I are getting a divorce that's why we moved. The love your father and I have for you both has not changed. I love you very much."

"What about Paul" Greg said. "You didn't answer me."

"Paul is very special to me. I am very fond of him. My relationship with him doesn't take away the love, devotion and responsibility I have as your mother. I hope you'll come to know Paul better and see why I want him apart of my life. He could have a place in yours, also. It's up to you."

"What about marriage?" Greg asked again.

"It's a possibility. I have to get through the divorce first."

"What about children?" Greg said.

"It will only make our family larger," Marni said squeezing her sons' shoulders. "There's lots of love to go around. Trust me."

"Yeah, the Brady bunch," Neil said.

"Not quite," Paul said. "I don't have any kids but if I do I want them just like you. Who could ask for a better mother than yours?"

"I'll make you a promise," Marni said. "You guys will be the first to know any plans made. How's that?" Marni leaned over and kissed each of her sons. Greg turned his eyes back to the screen. She guessed the inquisition was over that was a good sign. A big explosion was seen on the television screen. "Gotcha," Greg said to Paul. "I won. It's Neil's turn to play." Play was as usual, Marni thought, their curiosity had been satisfied and it gave them a sense of security. She had achieved her goal as a mother for the present.

"Follow me," Paul whispered. He led her into the small powder room off the main entryway. She closed the door behind them, and punched in the lock button. He slipped his arms around her, smothering her with kisses. "Here" Marni said. "Are you thinking of doing it here?" Paul gave Marni one of his wonderful smiles.

"We can give it the good old college try." Then he looked around. "On second thought, I don't think so." She kissed him again and his tongue lightly massaged her lips. "I love you very much." Marni rested her head against Paul's shoulder. "I love you too, but I feel so bad for the kids. They're getting zapped from all directions." He rubbed her head, slowly moving the palm of his hand. It eased some of her tension. "They'll get through it with some scars," Paul said, "but they could be alot deeper without you. You're one terrific mother." "Thanks," she said enjoying his closeness. He lifted her chin. "I'm with you every step of the way," he said lovingly, "for you . . . Greg and Neil." Her dark brown eyes filled with tears. Their lips met. Marni thought timing was so important in life.

Chapter Seventeen

The walls of the barroom were covered with mirrors reflecting faces of the crowd. A constant hum of voices competed with stereo speakers carrying the music of Diana Ross singing a medley of her hits. Neon rods of green and shocking pink ran across a wood molding capping off glass shelves loaded with liquor bottles. "There's a certain excitement about a restaurant when it first opens," Marni said. "Just look around, Nina. You'll see what I mean." Nina closed her eyes for a second. "I don't have to look around. I feel the vibes. It was a good idea to go out to dinner," Nina said. "I needed a break from working." Marni was glad that Nina agreed to the dinner date. "The chef's specialty is seafood," Marni said, "but the owner better learn how to operate this place. I never mind standing in the bar for a drink but it seems to me with this crowd it's more than just one. I'm annoyed." Nina put up her hand like she was stopping traffic. "Relax, drink slowly," Nina said. "Eventually we'll get a table." Marni listened to what Nina said and took a healthy swig of her drink. "If I were late for an appointment, the customer wouldn't wait," Marni complained. "But look around the bar, we're packed in like sardines. I guess, it depends where you have to wait."

"It's fun," Nina said poking Marni's side. "Lighten up. Listen to the chatter. Maybe we'll meet someone interesting."

"That's not my style getting picked up at a bar," Marni said. "Besides I'm involved."

"Paul?" Nina asked.

"Yes. Keep your fingers crossed. We've taken our friendship into serious territory."

"He's a great guy. I'm happy for you."

"Thanks," Marni said but this wasn't what she wanted to discuss with Nina. There was something else but she would have to be careful approaching the topic. She didn't want Nina to think that she was butting into someone else's business. "Nina, do you remember Kimberly telling us about her husband?" Nina shook her head yes. "The whole thing sounded very ominous," she said. "I spent the evening with Candy when Kimberly had a date with Henry. I got to know her. You might say, we really hit it off. If I hadn't been so involved finishing one piece and starting another, I would have called you. She told me something shocking. I'm concerned about them." Marni knew that it could be only one thing. "I think I know what you're going to say." Without hesitation Nina said, "Candy was raped by her father?" She grimaced in disgust before continuing. "He was drunk and thought she was Kimberly. Sick, huh."

"My stomach just did a flip flop," Marni said. "Kimberly told me the night Candy landed in the hospital. She hates George. I would say irrationally so, but I'm not a therapist, just my lay opinion."

"When you took her around for a rental what was she like?"

"Upset. Always concerned about Candy. How was she after she moved into the rental house?"

"Things seemed to settle down. At least, I thought so."

"Marni, the kid was so honest when I was with her. We never stopped talking. I feel we bonded. She told me that she would do some crazy thing after seeing her father. She's like a stick of dynamite, one flick of the switch. Whamo!"

"The move to Soundview was an attempt for Kimberly and Candy to move forward in their lives. How can they? Neither of them can maintain normalcy in their lives with George in the world. Kimberly gave her hate a new address, and that's all she did. It doesn't help Candy. She told me everything about George and herself. It's a horror story. It sure puts my divorce from Don in perspective. You know the old saying if everyone throws their troubles in the middle of the room, you'll take yours back. Without a doubt I would."

"We're two bright women. If we put our heads together, we ought to be able to help them."

"I've been thinking about this. It's probably a good idea to keep having dinners with them. Invite them to our homes as much as possible. Maybe it'll give them a strong sense that we're there for them. Kimberly and Candy are going to therapy and I'm sure Henry is on Kimberly's case. He's intuitive. Right now, there are a few positive forces all working at once perhaps for the first time in their lives. Let's hope it'll make a difference. What do you think, Nina?"

"In theory, what you said sounds good but it can only work if she would let go of the past. That's the tough part. I sympathize with her. Since Pierre, every man has been just another escape from my hurt. You know something, my pain didn't ease. All it did was waste alot of my time. Pierre is a wonderful memory and that's all he is. George is Kimberly's worst nightmare. What we both must do is move on. We've got to help her do that."

"We'll talk to her," Marni suggested, "but not during a dinner with Candy. I'll put together some kind of meeting for the three of us, in the next week or so. It's worth a try." Nina shook her head. "The life they're leading now is a no win situation," she said. "Whatever we do, it is better than nothing." Marni frowned. "Hate is the devil in disguise," she declared. "Kimberly did tell us there was an evil spirit in her life. Hopefully," Marni added, "we can show her it's of her own making." Nina finished her drink. "We'll give it our best shot," she replied. "That's all we can do."

Nina looked at her empty glass. "I need a refill. Do you?" Marni glanced at the still crowded room. "I'll battle my way to the bar. It's my turn to buy." She squeezed her body through one group of people after another, nodding to a few familiar faces. Reaching the bar, she immediately caught the eye of the bartender. "One very dry martini and an Absolute gimblet on the rocks, light on the lime juice and don't forget the lime peel."

"Coming right up," the bartender said.

On the way back, the crowd had thinned and it was easier for Marni to reach Nina. "Here," said Marni handing Nina her drink. "Did you do your usual badgering of the bartender?" Nina asked. Marni made an annoyed face. "Of course," she said thinking Nina had her number. "And?" Marni tasted her drink.

"It's perfect," she answered. "One time," Nina said, "the bartender is going to hand you the bottle and say make your own, lady. I hope I'm there. It'll be a pisser."

"If someone does that, I won't leave a tip."

"Sometimes you can be a real bitch."

"Don't talk about my bartenders when you flaunt your gallery of men. No one is sacred on your wall."

"But that's having a good time, Marni. Painting is my passion. It makes my ticker go. Sex makes everything else go, but I've reformed. Sex for sex sake is not part of my life anymore. I'm not seeing Alan, anymore. We parted ways. There'll be no diversions from my art except times like this, with a friend or until I meet my dream man."

"Do you think you can maintain your celibacy?" Marni said. "Even priests and nuns have a problem."

"I'll stand in front of my gallery and masturbate. You at least have Paul now?"

Marni smiled. "It's something wonderful. I wish it happens to you." And everyone else, she thought. "I do too," Nina replied. "Maybe you should clone him. I'd like someone to talk to, hold my hand, and walk with me on the beach. I'm ready to open my heart." Marni thought that was the first step. It was really the biggest one that she had to take. After that, everything fell into place and she was swept away. "Let's make a toast to that," said Marni holding her glass out. "But I'm not sure of the cloning." The women touched glasses.

Nina waved toward the entrance.

"Who's that?" Marni asked, wondering if it was one of her many admirers.

"I'm surprised you don't recognize him. You've just mentioned my famous wall."

Marni took a closer look. "You're right, the politician."

"Hello, Douglas," Nina said, brushing her cheek against his.

"Nina, nice to see you," Douglas replied. "You're looking as beautiful as ever."

"Douglas Stone," Nina said, "I would like you to meet Marni Taylor."

"It's a pleasure meeting you," Douglas said, shaking Marni's hand.

"And you," Marni said.

"Douglas," Nina said, "how is the campaign going?"

"Very well. There's good support for my candidacy. I have your vote, don't I, Nina?" Marni thought, he definitely still had a thing for Nina. By Nina's reaction, she had picked up on it.

"Not only my vote but my talent. Let me know if I should make circulars from your portrait."

"I'll give that some thought," Douglas said. "Thanks for the idea. Well, I'm being summoned. Good seeing you, Nina." He kissed her on the cheek. "And nice meeting you, Marni."

"Same here," Marni said. "Good luck with your campaign." Douglas gave Nina's hand an extra squeeze. "It really was wonderful seeing you again," he said. "I won't forget your idea." Marni wondered if Douglas knew he was being manipulated.

"By the way, Doug," Nina said, "did I mention that I removed your clothes in the portrait?"

"You what?" Douglas said. "Tell me you're kidding."

"Don't you need all the exposure that you can get, right, honey?" Nina asked. Marni watched Douglas's rosy cheeks turn a ghostly white. Poor guy, she thought. Marni awarded Nina, the Olympic Gold Medal for shattering the male ego.

"Your table is ready," the manager said. "Sorry for the delay." "We also have to go, Douglas," Nina said. "See you around." Nina laughed all the way to the table. After the women were seated Marni said, "The poor man is going home to have a heart attack. How could you?" Marni couldn't believe what Nina did. She definitely had nerve.

"I'm sure that he knows I was kidding," Nina said laughingly. "Don't be so sure," Marni said picking up the menu. "Oh, who cares anyway. I'm starved. Let's order quickly."

Chapter Eighteen

Marni entered the library. "That's that," she said slapping her hands together for a done deal. "Bonita is showing him around. I'd say he's a good replacement for Alex." By the facial expressions of Kimberly and Nina seated on the gray couch, Marni thought they agreed. She walked over to the bar and filled her glass with water. "His references checked out," Kimberly said. "He seems to know alot about shrubs and things."

"Who knows where Alex is now?" Nina said. "He cleaned out his quarters and vanished. He hasn't been seen since Candy was taken to the hospital."

"It doesn't matter," Kimberly said. "Alex saved Candy's life.

"How's Candy doing?" Nina asked.

"Okay," Kimberly said. "But how long is anyone's guess. Look what happened after she spent the evening with you. She said it was super talking to you but that didn't keep her from flipping out."

"We did hit it off," Nina said. "She has alot going for her."

"Candy has to believe that," Kimberly said taking a deep breath. "My life is one big roller coaster ride and so is hers."

"Experiences can only make you stronger," Marni said to Kimberly. She sat on the sofa opposite the two women. That was the reason Marni set up the meeting. The goal was to persuade Kimberly to positively use her experiences. Marni knew it was always easier to see the mistakes of others but she wanted to try if not for just Candy's sake.

"Stronger . . . well . . . , " Kimberly said, "I did leave home against my father's wishes. It took some stamina to traipse around New York looking for employment but once I found a job I did work myself up the corporate ladder. Quite successfully. George selected my renderings for his office building. We worked together on the project. It was a comfort to know that I would see him regularly. It was easy being with him. There came a time when I thought that I loved him. He was a polite person. What did I know? Completely inexperienced. Constantly having men paw me. Hearing the ridiculous comments made to me by men as they passed me in a hallway of a building or on the street. It's tough being part of the Manhattan scene when you're from a small town. Marriage to George seemed like a good idea. Then I watched him change before my eyes. The pressures of business egged him on to drink frequently. I stood by him waiting for him to stop, but it never happened. He was just repeating an old pattern of his. One I knew nothing about until after my life and Candy's was ruined. When I asked him for a divorce, he lost it. He raped me and later that night he raped Candy." Kimberly took another deep breath. "It was the lowest point in my life because I didn't protect my daughter by leaving George sooner. I tried to pull my life together and Candy's with therapy. I think everything will be fine. Then George shows up. Yes, I managed to build up a successful business and still keep on expanding it. But it doesn't compensate for my pain. It's really my escape. So what do you want me to learn from my experience? I made a mistake marrying George. Why didn't I do a background check on him before saying yes? I shouldn't talk to strangers. My mistake was to allow for his behavior but I won't make that mistake with Candy. I'm trying to stay on top of her but George blows it all apart. Don't you see that? What should I do? Tell me."

"First you can't dwell on the past," Nina said. "It won't change anything. What happened happened."

"I know that but I still can't stop thinking of it."

"You've got a chance now," Marni said.

"I thought so too, but then there's always George again."

"Move forward," Marni urged. "Before you allowed for George's behavior, now put limits on it. Work out a visiting schedule. Speak to his doctors and have them help him abide by it." Marni looked at Nina for her support. "Make peace," Nina said placing her hand on Kimberly's.

"Dr. Norris suggested George, Candy and I have therapy sessions together so we can co-exist. Henry thinks the same thing. I can't sit in the same room with him. I won't let Candy, either."

"It'll help," Marni said. "Trust me. I know."

"You don't know. Your daughter wasn't raped by her father."

"It happened, nothing can change that," Marni said. "Nothing."

"The hate won't help Candy either," Nina said. "It'll only hurt her more. Consider her reactions."

"Therapy with the three of you is the only answer," Marni said. "You'll work out a framework for functioning as a family. It'll take time but it's worth it."

"I don't want therapy with George," Kimberly said. "That's a closed issue."

"Did you ever think your attitude incites the situation?" Marni said. "What happened when you returned from Henry's house and found George there? Did you once consider anyone feelings but your own?"

"What are you saying Marni?"

"Did you walk into the room and assess what was happening?"

"I saw George and Candy in the room together and feared for Candy's well being. I wanted him to leave."

"It's always what you wanted," Marni said, "but Candy opened the door. The tone of Marni's voice was sharper but she still maintained control over her emotions. "Obviously, she wanted to work out what she was feeling with her father but you didn't let her. You've put her in the middle of the conflict and look what she does each time. Don't you see what I'm saying? For Candy's best interests, it's time to sit down with George. He's not going to go away." Kimberly's body stiffened. "He shouldn't be allowed to walk the streets," she said looking away from Marni. "He is though," Marni insisted. "Now deal with it. Call Dr. Norris let her arrange a meeting for the three of you. See how it goes."

"The situation isn't going to change overnight," Nina said, "but at least start the ball rolling. Show Candy there's some kind of hope for the future. Give her a fighting chance to survive. Come on now."

"A mother wants to protect her child," Marni said, "but that doesn't mean just by a shield. Give her the opportunity to understand what she's up against and then develop the skill to deal with it. With your support, she'll come out a winner."

"All of what you said makes sense," said Kimberly first glancing at Marni then Nina. "I just don't know if I can do it."

"You won't know until you start trying," Marni said. She felt that there was a slight awakening on Kimberly's part. "Nina and I will help you. Henry will too."

"Henry," Kimberly added softly, "he's definitely in my life." She smiled opening her green eyes wider.

"Do I detect a new glow in your eyes?" Nina said.

Kimberly nodded. She got up and walked to the bar where she filled a glass with brandy. Slowly, Kimberly drank some of it. Returning, she stood in front of the fireplace. "I . . . we . . . made love," she stammered.

"Are you still on Cloud Nine?" Marni said. She thought, this could be Kimberly's motivation to move on.

Kimberly closed her eyes. "Like nothing I could've imagined," Kimberly whispered. When she opened her eyes, she said in a more normal tone of voice, "Oh . . . I don't know if I can tell you about it."

"It's special to relive such moments," Nina said. "I know. I do it often enough."

Kimberly emptied her glass of brandy and took a deep breath. "He was so understanding," she said softly, "so considerate of my needs. We kissed until I was comfortable enough to take his hand, kiss his fingers and place them here." She rested her hand on her breast. Her voice grew louder. "It was an important moment and he knew this. He asked if I was sure. I covered his hand with mine. He promised to stop whenever I wished." Kimberly looked first to Marni and then Nina. The only noise heard was the crackling of the firewood. "It had been so natural to be with him, so beautiful. I didn't feel sinful or evil or overwhelmed with negative feelings. It wasn't this way with George. My body responded. I know what I've been missing all these years. You were right, making love with the right man is wonderful."

"I'm starting over," Marni said, "with Paul. The intimate

part of my life is over with Don but the contact with him will never stop. He's the father of my children. A fact I can't change. I have to work with him to give the kids a strong feeling that they still have two parents concerned with their welfare. He's not reliable all the time and it's frustrating as hell so I fill the void the best I can. I don't fill it with hate. It'll only hurt the kids. Don has to form his own relationship with Greg and Neil. Give George that opportunity, if not alone with Candy then under supervision. Think about it. Take this horrible pressure off your shoulders so you can enjoy life, that's why you moved to Soundview, to start over. What better way than a new relationship with Henry to make it more fulfilling." Marni got up and stood next to Kimberly, "Make a pack with me, we'll look to the future together. Will you?"

"You're ridiculous to compare George to Don," Kimberly lashed out at Marni. Kimberly walked back to the bar and refilled her glass. "If he stays away from us," she said, "everything will be fine." Marni was taken back by Kimberly's harsh words but followed her to the bar. "As long as he's living," Marni said, "there's the possibility he'll see Candy. You're kidding yourself if you think otherwise."

"Oh, we've been through this," said Nina. Her voice filled with frustration. "For how long will things be okay? It doesn't seem to me that he's willing to stop seeing Candy."

"See what I told you," Kimberly said angrily, "court orders mean nothing." Marni grasped Kimberly's shoulders making sure Kimberly at least had to face her although she still had the option to tune out what she was saying. "Then protect yourself and Candy," Marni responded quickly, "sit with him. Talk with him." Nina got up and joined Kimberly and Marni. Nina put her arm around Kimberly's shoulder, "Marni is right," Nina said. "Look how far you've come. Did you ever expect Henry in your life?" Kimberly without saying a word removed Nina's arm and returned to the couch. Marni exchanged looks with Nina thinking what more could they possibly say.

Chapter Nineteen

The light turned green. Kimberly pressed her foot on the gas pedal and continued her drive to Candy's school. Lately, she thought things were working out. Since Candy started seeing Dr. Norris again, she and Candy were good together. They were talking, sharing the happenings of the day, and continuing to work on interior design projects. Kimberly was especially thankful that her relationship had grown to a level where Candy was telling her how she spends her leisure time with friends. She never set up an appointment with Dr. Norris for George, Candy and herself. She couldn't bring herself to do that and besides everything was fine without it.

Driving along Kimberly inhaled the sweet spring air filled with with fragrances of lilac and rose bushes and fresh cut grass. It rejuvenated her. She felt good about herself. An intimacy was growing between her and Henry that Dr. Norris thought was very positive. A few times she made love with Henry and each time it was better. She now anticipated the intimacy and wanted it. Her hand slipped inside her coat and touched her nipples, now hard for the right reasons.

She pulled through the school's metal gates and entered the private road, eagerly looking forward to her drive home with her daughter. Candy had slept at a friend's the night before to study for a French exam. Kimberly turned onto the circular driveway in front of the school building obeying the fifteen miles an hour speed limit. She hoped for a parking spot near the school entrance but all she saw was George leaning against his car twenty feet away. Why does he have to spoil my day? I'll show him what I mean when I say stay away from Candy.

She leaned forward. Instinctively, her hands gripped the steering wheel, turning her knuckles white. Pressing her foot against the gas pedal, she quickly increased the speed level to reach her target. A horn blasted. Brakes screeched. A male voice shouted, "Hey lady, watch where you're going." She plunked down her foot on the brakes, just missing a fender. "Do you want to kill someone?" the same voice shouted. Ignoring the words, her eyes followed George's movements. He bolted for the driver's door of the car and fled the scene. Embarrassed, she kept her eyes focused straight ahead and moved the car forward. The more roadway between her and the passenger of the car that she cut off eliminated the possibility of a verbal exchange. A space at the curb opened up, she slid in and turned off the ignition. Her body was wet with perspiration; her clothes stuck to her skin. She shuddered as a wave of chills swept over her clammy skin; she pulled her collar close to her neck and then looked at her trembling hands. I could have killed him, she thought. My god, I could have killed him. Tears filled her eyes trickling down her cheek. She leaned her head against the headrest. Grasping the welting of the seat so her hands wouldn't shake, Kimberly closed her eyes. She was grateful for a few quiet minutes before her daughter arrived.

"Hi, Mom," Candy said, sliding into the front seat.

"Hi, Candy," Kimberly responded weakly.

"You look terrible," Candy said. "What's wrong?"

"I almost hit a car," Kimberly said. "I'll be okay. Come on, honey, shut the door. Let's go home."

The drive back was endless. She imagined each passing car was a near miss for a head on collision. Kimberly maintained a speed of thirty miles an hour. Finally passing through the gates of Soundview, she welcomed the tall pine trees and sighed.

Kimberly passed her door and stopped the car. Dragging herself out of the car, she walked slowly into her home. She stared at the phone and decided to call Henry. Her ear was glued to the receiver, listening to the rings, waiting to be connected, but her eyes followed Candy up the stairs. She knew this was Henry's day off. When she heard his voice, Kimberly blurted out, "Henry, I almost ran over George with my car." Upon hearing those words with her own ears, she feared the consequences. The receiver quivered in her sweaty hand.

"Where are you?" Henry asked calmly.

"I'm home," Kimberly mumbled. "I just came back from picking up Candy at school."

"I'll be right over."

Kimberly put down the telephone, walked over to the service cart, and poured herself a brandy from the crystal decanter. She dropped down on the sofa totally exhausted. Her body slouched against the cushions and her mind a prisoner of her thoughts.

"Mom do you like these sketches?" Candy asked. Kimberly feeling, her daughter's hand on her arm was suddenly brought back to the present. "I'm sorry," Kimberly said seeing Candy in front of her for the first time. "What did you say?" Candy moved the papers in front of her mother again. "I asked if you like these sketches." Candy touched her mother's forehead. "Are you all right Mom?" Kimberly took hold of the sketches with her free hand. "I'm fine, just fine," she said sitting up straight and putting her drink on the coffee table. "I'm waiting for Henry." Kimberly studied the drawings. Candy, at the suggestion of Dr. Norris, was helping Kimberly design a bedroom for a client's daughter. She and Dr. Norris hoped Candy's self-image would improve through the development of her creative talent. Kimberly was looking to strengthen the bond between them. "These are great," Kimberly said. "The work of a professional."

Candy sat next to her mother. "You think so?" Candy said.

"I'm really proud of you," Kimberly replied running her finger across the paper helping her to focus on it. She kissed her daughter's cheek. "Our client will love them." Kimberly held up the sketches again. "Your selection of color and fabrics is perfect, but part of our job is to offer a choice of two or three decorating suggestions. Look through some fabric books in my study, and then put together two other ideas. When that's done, we'll set up an appointment with the client. How's that, honey?"

"Thanks, Mom." Candy took her papers and was about to go upstairs when the gate buzzer sounded. "Mom," Candy said, "that must be Henry."

"Please buzz him in. Thanks."

Candy did as her mother requested, then mounted the steps two at time. "I can't wait for the meeting!" She yelled back.

The doorbell rang. Kimberly remained on the couch self-conscious of her misdeed earlier in the day. For a few seconds she delayed opening the door for Henry. She wandered how it would affect his feelings toward her. The doorbell rang again. She hoped since Henry was a psychiatrist he would understand her action and not let that be the reason to end their relationship. He warned her that she had to control her emotions or else they would get her in trouble. Wasn't this what Marni and Nina was trying to tell her but she refused to hear? How right they all were. She would make that appointment with Dr. Norris and accept responsibility of making a terrible situation worse. Again she heard the bell. This time she opened the door. "Henry, I'm so thankful you're here." It wasn't Henry at the door step. "George, what are you doing here?"

Pushing Kimberly aside, George stalked into the foyer. "I want to see Candy. Right now!" he demanded. "You can't keep me from my daughter any longer." Kimberly didn't want Candy to hear George's voice. Energized by fear, Kimberly ran through the living room and into the kitchen. "I'm calling Theodore," she shouted and picked up the phone. "Go ahead," George said entering the kitchen. "It won't do any good this time." What was he saying? She looked in his face for some clue. "What do you mean?"

"He's dead," George said. "It's not possible," she said hoping to see some sign he was lying. "I just spoke to him only a week ago."

"My dear Theodore Freemont stopped me from seeing Candy too often." George slid a pistol out of his pocket. "What's that for?" Kimberly shouted. "Just leave George." She pointed to the kitchen door. "Haven't you done enough to Candy and me? Please go quietly."

"I'm taking Candy with me."

"No. You're not." Candy screamed, running into the room. "I hate you." She threw the sketches that she was holding in his face, and caught him off guard.

Kimberly grabbed Candy's arm and ran out the kitchen

door. Thankful for the woods nearby, Kimberly led Candy through the densely treed area. She made sure the trunks of the tree protected them until they reached the guest-house door. Kimberly and Candy quickly went inside. Kimberly locked the door behind them and then shoved her daughter behind the sofa. Not hearing George's movements outside, she picked up the receiver of the telephone. There was no tone. Furiously she pressed the button but it didn't activate a tone. Despondently, she realized that she had chosen the wrong way. George's heavy footsteps grew louder on the brick path. She rejoined Candy and squeezed her tightly. Chancing a peek from behind the sofa she saw George peering through the front window.

"Stay down Mom," Candy said. "He'll see you."

Kimberly ducked her head and crouched lower, pulling Candy with her.

George rattled the doorknob. "Open this door, Kimberly," he commanded, banging on the door with his gun. "I'm warning you."

"I'm scared Mom," Candy whispered. "He's going to kill us."

He moved around the guest-house and tried lifting every locked window. Kimberly clutched Candy tightly; she felt their hearts pounding. The doorknob rattled again. Suddenly a shot rang out and George burst into the room. The women were instantly enveloped in the naked violence of his rage.

"I know you're here, Kimberly," George shouted. "You ran away from me once, taking Candy with you, but you won't run away again."

"Stay down," Kimberly whispered. Then she stood and walked from behind the sofa to face George. "Is this how you show your love, George?" Kimberly asked, her voice quaking from fear and anger.

"You left me no choice. I needed you. I needed my daughter. You took away everything I had that was worthwhile." George's face streaked with tears. "Today you even tried to kill me. Why Kimberly? I told you I was sorry for what I did."

"What?" Candy exclaimed, standing up. "I don't believe it."

"I'm not lying, Candy. Your mother tried to run me down in

front of your school. Didn't you, Kimberly? Tell Candy." Candy looked at the floor. "I know it's true. Mother why didn't you tell me?"

"I hate him so much," Kimberly ranted staring at Candy, "for what he did to you . . . for what he did to all of us. Even so, I couldn't kill him. I just wanted to scare him so he wouldn't come around anymore. That's all."

"Oh, Mom. . . . "

"George," Kimberly said, "please listen. I couldn't harm you. I was angry and so frustrated. Every time Candy and I were doing okay you returned and then Candy wouldn't be herself." Kimberly's words came out softly. "I'm sorry for what I did. It was stupid." She took a few steps toward him but she stopped when he shook the gun. She thought it was a warning to stay back. "We'll work it out. Please put the gun down." She saw him lower the weapon and decided to walk slowly toward him. "We'll go to therapy together, just like you said. I'm sorry, George. I'm so sorry. . . . "

"I just wanted us to be together again," George wailed.

Clustered beads of sweat dripped down his face. "You ruined it, Kimberly, just like you ruined everything." She listened to his words but stared at the gun pointed at her.

Kimberly knew she had to control her voice. Her actions today had pushed him over the edge. It was up to her to bring him back for Candy's sake. She took several steps toward him. "Everything will be fine," she said. "Nothing's ruined. We're going to work it out. I promise. Please give me the gun for Candy's sake." She took a few more steps. "Don't do this. Give me the gun." She was now standing close to him. "I'm sorry George." Kimberly tried to take the gun from his hand. George squeezed the trigger. Kimberly slumped to the floor.

Chapter Twenty

A young woman, her golden hair and white gown glowed in the eerie light illuminated by the moon. She wandered down a dark road. Its circuitous route took her by a copse of barren trees. Her dark eyes had a haunted look. She held her hands up like shutters in attempt to avoid the sight along the road. It was an unyielding cycle, repeated. There were bloody babies spewing forth from the bowels of the trees, only to be destroyed by umbilical-like tentacles attached to the same birthing trees. There was no place to escape. She was trapped. "Mommy . . . Mommy. . . . !" Her cry echoed unanswered. Splotches of red suddenly appeared across her young body. She crumpled to the ground, lying in the same fetal position as the vulnerable babies next to her, totally exposed to the predators of the dark. An ambulance appeared from nowhere and screeched to a halt by her side, its sirens blasting.

Nina jumped up from the chair, startled by the sound of the siren still attacking her ears. A glance at her watch revealed Nina had been sleeping for a few hours. It was mid-morning. Looking around the private room, she still thought that it was drab except the Miro print across from Candy's hospital bed. She walked over to the window and opened the blinds surprised to see a sign saying Emergency Room on a brick wall facing her. Something she didn't notice late in the night when she and Candy became occupants of the room.

"Mmm," Candy groaned and Nina immediately went to her side.

She saw a small, motionless figure lay beneath the white hospital sheet and an IV tube attached to her arm. How pathetic, Nina thought. "Candy," Nina said, "you're okay. Can you hear me, honey? You're okay. The bullet was removed from your side. You'll be fine." Candy's eyes flickered open for no more than a second and then she fell back to sleep. While Nina stayed near the bed making sure Candy was asleep, she realized how stiff her muscles were from the uncomfortable chair. She stretched her arms and rotated her upper body trying to limber up. After awhile, Nina left her vigil and went near the window. She continued stretching slowly, breathing deeply, and then began to do aerobic exercises. She held the window sill for support and lifted each of her legs alternately in three positions. Then she stretched out on the floor resting her back on the cold tiles. While supporting her head with her arms, she lifted her head and opposite knee simultaneously for two sets of ten. Her favorite exercise was to pretend she was bicycling by rotating her feet in the air. Afterwards Nina cooled down with some stretching again.

When she collapsed in the chair, she was tired but the aches and stiffness were gone. Nina listened to the usual hospital sounds emanating from the hallway—the clatter of wheeled carts, the whoosh of swinging doors, and the chattering of nurses. Every so often, there was a blast from an ambulance siren. Sometime in the early afternoon, Nina was joined by Marni carrying all the things on Nina's list: a change of clothing, some toiletries, her sketching supplies, and Candy's cassette player with tapes. Familiar music was often soothing. Last night she tried to think of everything while she was on the telephone with Marni informing her the surgery went well. Nina, not wanting to disturb Candy with conversation, placed two chairs in front of the window and left Marni sitting there while she changed. A few moments passed before Nina sat next to Marni. "That's better." she said softly. "Sure is convenient to have a bathroom in the room."

"It's really for the patient's use only," Marni said.

"Who'll know?" Nina replied. "Anyhow, I'm starting to feel almost human again. But then who the hell wants to be part of the human race, if George was a member?" Nina sat on the chair draping her foot over the arm. "Who cares about him, anyway?" she said. "He won't harm anyone again. George made sure of that by blowing his brains out."

"It's mind boggling the events of the last twenty four

hours," Marni said giving Nina a copy of a newspaper. "Here," she said, "I thought you'd be interested. At least, it didn't make the front page. Turn to page three." Nina skimmed the page. She thought she didn't have to waste anytime on the article. Unfortunately, she had a front row seat. "All the names were spelled correctly. I'm thrilled. Now tell me. How are your kids dealing with this?"

"They're very upset but at least they didn't see anything. The police are keeping the area off limits. I didn't let them go to school today. They're spending the day at my parents' house."

"That was a good idea."

"Poor Bonita. There are police officers roaming the property and forget the reporters. Her phone hasn't stopped ringing. I bet, she's sorry Alan had one installed with her own listed number. Forget my phone. The tape broke from all the messages. Well, what can you do?"

"Just take the phone off the hook." Nina knew Marni wouldn't. "I'll see," said Marni. Nina thought that response was a polite 'no.' Marni's business depended on the phone.

"I was thinking," Marni said, "let's raze the guest-house when we can."

"Fine with me," Nina quickly responded. "I'll drive the bulldozer. We don't need it staring us in the face."

"I'm glad you agree." Marni pushed her hair behind her ears.

"What are you thinking?" Nina asked. She knew Marni's hair adjustment meant serious stuff. "I'm feeling guilty putting the investment together." Nina couldn't believe what she just heard. Since Nina believed it was a great move for her. Her involvement with Kimberly and Marni and the kids gave her something more than her painting. Nina thought, how could Marni possibly feel the way she did? Marni had family in her life whom she cared about. "Don't blame yourself," Nina said. "It might have been for a short time but our friendship meant something to each of us, including Kimberly."

"Not enough," Marni said. "She's dead."

"Well, there's a bright side. Candy won't be alone now. I'm here. You're here. See, you put together a new family."

"That's true," Marni said. She had put the deal together for her self-serving purposes. If Nina thought otherwise, it eased Marni's conscience. "Did Candy wake up?"

"She opened her eyes for a second, but that's all. I don't know if she's aware of anything. It hasn't been much time since the operation."

"We'll take shifts," Marni suggested. She wanted to do her share. "Four hours on, four hours off."

"No. I'll stay the whole time," Nina said glancing at Candy. By the time Candy came out of surgery, Nina had made her decision. It would surprise Marni. She wouldn't call herself exactly mother material. "I've been thinking these past hours, about myself, and about Candy. She has no one else. I want to be there for her. I'm going to ask her to live with me." Marni leaned forward to be closer to Nina. "Don't be ridiculous," Marni said. "It's too much. You two hit it off. But taking on the sole responsibility for her well being that's something else." Nina didn't think that at all. She was more concerned with her ability to set a good example. "You've got the kids . . . and Paul. I'll be fine." Nina believed with George gone Candy had a good chance to lead a normal life if she worked out her feelings about Kimberly's death. She agreed with Marni that Candy wanted to reach out to George and make some kind of peace with him. She liked being a normal kid without using drugs and running around with boys in her school. Nina was also counting on Dr. Norris's expertise to guide her.

"Bringing up kids is tough. You have no idea what's involved. Until this moment, you had to only take care of Nina. Am I right? Now a kid with Candy's problems," Marni added. "Can I say anything to dissuade you?"

"My mind is made up," Nina answered. Nina saw Marni relax her body against the back of the chair. She knew that Marni was finished trying to change her mind. "You'll need lots of help," Marni finally said. "I'll have it," Nina assured her. "I'm counting on you. Henry. And Dr. Norris."

"Speaking of Dr. Norris," said Marni, "would you like me to call her?"

"Would you?" Nina responded. She would've done it herself but she really didn't want to leave Candy.

"Be right back," Marni said standing.

Nina sat looking out the window and intermittently at Candy. She opened her sketch pad to a clean page needing a release for her emotions. However her hand holding, the pencil didn't move. The page was still blank when Marni returned.

"Sorry to take so long," she said softly joining Nina. "Dr. Norris wanted to know every detail."

"I couldn't tell you how long you were gone. I've been staring at a blank piece of paper. I can't do anything. Artist's block."

"How about just being exhausted? Too tired to think. Why don't you go home? Take my car and I'll stay with Candy."

"No. I don't want to leave. Forget this," Nina said closing the sketch pad and putting it in her bag with her pencil. "Tell me what Dr. Norris said."

"She was very upset, naturally. She's been their therapist for ages. I told her what your intentions were. Don't be surprised if she questions your reasons. It's in Candy's best interests, a therapist looking after her patient."

"I understand," said Nina nodding her head in agreement. "I'll be open to her suggestions. Don't worry." Nina quickly patted Marni's hand. "I'll tread lightly."

"If she only listened to us, all of this could've been avoided," Marni declared. She shook her head. "What a total waste of a life. It had to be stressful supervising the renovation and decoration of Soundview. Afterall, she was going to live there, too, and you don't want to hear constant complaints. The three of us never had any kind of conflict, and all our nerves were surely stretched to the limit. Why couldn't some of this rational behavior spill over to her relationship with George? He was Candy's father."

"It's not my thing to be a Monday morning-quarterback," Nina said. "But I would have simply made some ground rules. I was so frustrated hearing Kimberly say all George had to do was stay away. She was the problem also. The family sessions would have helped all of them. Didn't you work out an agreement with Don?"

Nina sighed. "What's the use?"

"You know," said Marni, "she really didn't know how fortunate she was to have something going with Henry. If she did, she wouldn't have tried to run George down. I can't imagine being so angry to do that to Don."

"Different history. I never thought of doing away with Pierre's wife either. Anger and hate really does a number to your insides and we've just seen the proof."

"Let's change the subject for a while," Marni said touching Nina's knee. "Guess who's pregnant?"

"Barbara," Nina answered.

"You're a psychic."

"How's this going to affect your divorce?"

"It'll probably be the catalyst we needed to get things moving. I spoke to my attorney and informed him of the situation. He promised to take action immediately. I hope he keeps his promise. I want to get on with my life."

"Do the boys know?"

"Yes. They were very upset."

"What happens if I marry Paul and we have a child together? Can you just imagine?"

"Your kids are afraid of being more neglected by their father. He drops in and out of their lives like a yo-yo. You've always been there for them. Paul seems like a stand up sort of guy. He did a good job with the closing. He was charming at the party. You looked like you were glad he was there. What can I say? How do I know what kind of husband he'll be or for that matter a father? You're the one who goes way back with him. What do you think?"

"Paul is something else." Marni looked at Candy, guilty to be happy when Candy was in such pain. "He's an incredible human being."

"There's your answer. Marrying Paul doesn't sound much of a risk to me."

There was a moan from the bed. Nina rose and quickly went to Candy's side. Candy was tossing her head on the pillow; her fingers clenched the blanket. Nina wiped Candy's forehead with a moist cool cloth while Candy whimpered, "Mommy . . . Mommy." Nina was shakened when the whimpers quickly escalated into howls and she urged Marni to get help. A nurse administered a tranquilizing shot. Within a few moments, Candy began to sleep again and Nina and Marni went back to the chairs near the window. Nina knew she would have to get use to this but was grateful for Marni's presence this time. The remainder of the day was spent with quiet chatter, Nina reading the paper and Marni reading her book. When it got dark, Marni went to the cafeteria and bought some juice, a yogurt and a muffin for Nina's dinner. Then Marni left promising to call Nina later.

Nina was glad for the time alone. She napped, ate the food and tried to focus in on her sketch pad. When Henry arrived she had two figures filling the once blank paper. Henry stood quietly, holding a floral arrangement and looked over Nina's shoulder. She knew that he was reluctant to disturb her concentration. Finally, Nina looked up and smiled. "What lovely flowers," she said.

"How's our girl doing?" Henry asked. "She woke up once and became hysterical," Nina said, approaching Candy's bed with Henry. He put the flowers on the nightstand. "The nurse sedated her after that. Do you think she remembered what happened?" Nina asked. She stuck her finger in the vase making sure there was water. "Probably," Henry responded. "At least she's not denying reality.

"I spoke to her therapist and she'll be here first thing in the morning." Nina added more water to the vase from the water pitcher. "Marni called Dr. Norris, too. We thought, it was a good idea. If Candy is up tomorrow, she might find some comfort with her presence."

"How are you doing?" he asked. "Have you had anything to eat today?"

"I'm fine," Nina said.

"Were you planning to spend the night again?"

"Of course, I don't want Candy to be alone."

"I thought you might feel that way, and I agree. She shouldn't be alone. I hired a private nurse for the night shift. I'm taking you to dinner and then home, doctor's orders."

"Seems like you thought of everything," said Nina feeling

relieved and very grateful. She could use the rest at home. After many assurances by Henry and the nurse that Candy would sleep through the night, Nina decided she could leave. She kissed Candy's forehead, smoothed her hair, and straightened out the sheets. Nina handed the nurse her phone number and finally walked out the door with Henry.

Chapter Twenty-One

Nina was upset with herself for not insisting Henry take her straight home. All she wanted was a hot bath and bed but Henry wanted dinner so she felt that she should keep him company. They were in the hospital cafeteria waiting on line to reach the food displays. Nina handed Henry a tray. "Thanks," he said. "The hospital food is pretty good." She sighed. "Make a choice for both of us." When they reached the food, Henry chose two spinach salads and two bottled waters. Nina returned her tray and followed Henry to an empty corner table in the dining room. Silently he set the food on the bright red formica tabletop while the frosted plastic tile above their heads became dark. Henry stood on the chair and poked the tile making it turn white. "We could have moved," Nina said as Henry sat. "All the lights flicker on and off one time or other."

Sitting across from Henry, Nina noticed his blood shot eyes and dark lines beneath his eyes. "Did you get any rest last night?" she asked. "Not too much. I'm still working through my state of shock. Helping people deal with impulsive behavior has been my life's work. Having it invade my private world, I can't stop asking myself alot of questions." She understood where he was coming from. She was also asking herself questions. What could she and Marni have done or said to change the course of events? Should she have become Kimberly's bodyguard? All the signs instigating Kimberly's behavior were there and she knew it. Throughout her life she, like Kimberly, rationalized impulsive behavior to such an extent that it became an on going pattern. It was a spring board to dive head first into a situation. Only recently Nina came to terms with this. Her lifestyle was a result of two very loving parents who made her feel anything was possible. Nina did whatever she wanted including falling in love with a man twice her age. Her lover used his love, wealth, and connections to keep her committed to a relationship where all she cared about was just being with him. She was crushed emotionally when her devotion was not enough to have him on her terms, a marriage like the one her mother and father shared. Once she left Pierre, she was only able to express her love on canvas. She and Kimberly were both consumed with excessive feelings. Nina was smothered with love while Kimberly was blown away by anger. It kept them from achieving normal lives for themselves. Her wanting to offer Candy a home was the coming together of two crippled lives, hers and Kimberly, and to make one whole. She hoped that she had grown enough to make her wise and strong enough to pull it off. Nina put a forkful of spinach into her mouth and studied Henry's face. How frustrated Henry must feel. He lost not only someone who was seeking his help, but a lover. This was the person who like Kimberly, Nina hoped would do everything possible to help her be successful in her course of action. Could he make sense out of this tragedy? Could he become her mentor? Was she asking too much?

"This morning I got some background on George," Henry said.

"Tell me," Nina said. "I'm interested."

"He was a teenager with problems," Henry began to explain, "heavy drinking, aggressive behavior leading to violence, and attempted suicide. He never really came to terms with the causes of his dysfunctional behavior. They were only suppressed and that's when Kimberly entered his life."

"I guess they rubbed salt on each others open wounds," Nina said softly. "Does it matter anymore who did what to whom? They left a bloodied daughter lying in a hospital bed alone." Henry didn't respond. He took out his cellular phone. "This is Dr. Gordon. How's she doing?" He was silent for a few seconds. "Thanks," he said looking across to Nina. "Candy is sleeping peacefully." He slipped the phone in his jacket pocket. "That's good news," Nina said. "Thanks for calling."

"I hope you're ready for a few rough days," Henry said. "The police want to finish their investigation by questioning Candy. The funeral isn't going to be easy to handle either. It's important to know these things and prepare yourself for them.

"I think that I'm mentally prepared," Nina said. "It's not just the rest of the week, Henry. I've decided that I want Candy to live with me. I want to be in her life as long as she wants me there." Nina wanted Henry to know her position. She thought that was the only way they could work together. It was important that he knew she would take his advice seriously and act upon his suggestions. Her initiative was the difference between her and Kimberly. The first step in the long road of Candy's recovery. "That's a heavy commitment," Henry said. "She's a very disturbed young lady." Nina felt his eyes search her soul. "I know all she's been through . . . she and Kimberly." Considering Henry's fragile state she didn't want to make him feel uncomfortable. Her knowledge of his intimacy with Kimberly wasn't mentioned. "Candy is going to need a great deal of support and therapy," he said. "Yes, I'm aware of her needs, which only makes me more determined. Who else does Candy have? Who else do I have? I can make a difference in her life."

"It seems to me you're filling some emptiness in your own life. That reason will get you into trouble. What happens if the road ahead is a tough one? You'll become extremely unhappy and frustrated." She doubted that. Her strong bond to her dead friend, Kimberly and her daughter, Candy, would motivate her to help Candy all she could. Nina could've explained her feelings better on canvas than with Henry now sitting across from her. "I'm aware of responsibility. My eyes are wide open entering the commitment." Why was Henry relentless with his prodding? Marni did say that he would help her face her inner being. "She might never recover from this," Henry said, "even if you give her everything that you can. Then what will you do? How will you cope?" Henry assumed the role of the devil's advocate but this made Nina more resolved to carry out what she thought was right for herself and Candy. "I'll have to cope, that's it. I believe that with help Candy will make a good life for herself. I'm committed."

"I see your mind is made up, and nothing I say will change it."

"Marni tried already but she couldn't either."

"There's alot involved becoming Candy's guardian. First, we have to ask her. If she favors it, papers have to be filed with the court asking for temporary guardianship. I'll help you all I can. You'll need Dr. Norris in your corner. Speak to her about it tomorrow."

"That means a lawyer." Nina wasn't thinking along legal lines at all. She thought that she would ask Candy to stay with her when she left the hospital. That's it. No long drawn out legal process. Now Henry is talking about lawyers and papers. She hoped it didn't become complicated. "Is all this necessary?" Nina asked.

"Absolutely," Henry answered. "Candy is a minor."

"Well, I'll speak to Marni and let her talk to Paul. Hopefully, he can do it or get someone. I guess you've taken up the role of administrator, first the nurse in the hospital and now this." Nina was beginning to see what it means to be responsible for another person. Thank god for Henry's guidance. She needed him. "I hope you don't mind," Nina said to Henry, "but I think I'm going to be depending alot on you."

"That's okay. If Candy agrees to live with you, it'll give her a sense of a home right away."

"Which is what she needs," said Nina putting the plastic lid on salad dish. "Henry, I think I'll take the salad with me. I'm not very hungry. Since you're finished, we can go."

"I'm ready," he said and stood. "The salad can be your lunch tomorrow." Though Nina was very tired, she realized Henry was making it easy for her to function. He knew her condition and she appreciated it. If she had any doubts about his capability to help her, she now felt foolish. This was a man who had boundless strength and sensitivity. Someone she could trust which was most important. He had helped her focus on what responsibility she was undertaking. It was one thing to make a decision and it was quite another thing to understand the ramifications. She felt not only had she changed her lifestyle but now she knew who would be functioning in it. This was the first time in her life that she was in touch with the real Nina Levin. The awareness would make her a better advocate for Candy and equally important it would give a new dimension to her artwork. Walking out of the dining room holding the plastic dish together, she remembered that she was going to dinner for his sake, that was a laugh. Once they reached Henry's car, Nina said, "If I fall asleep during the car ride, I apologize ahead time."

Chapter Twenty-Two

Nina was just about to enter Candy's hospital room when a short middle-aged woman dressed in a blue business suit walked out the door. "Excuse me," Nina said. "Are you Dr. Norris?" Nina smiled at the woman knowing it was. With the help of the supervisory nurse, she had timed her entrance well. By phoning from the cafeteria Nina knew the therapist's arrival. She gave Dr. Norris time to spend with Candy then headed upstairs. "Yes, I am," she replied. Nina immediately extended her hand. "I'm Nina Levin, Candy's friend. How's she doing today?" Nina already had a report on Candy's condition. She spoke to the night nurse before she went off duty in the morning. However, this was a good starting point for her conversation with the therapist. "Candy's in a great deal of pain," Dr. Norris said, "not all physical. I can assure you, but she's sleeping now." Nina sympathetically said, "I hear what your saying." She wanted this meeting to go well. "I was hoping that I would see you this morning, Dr. Norris.

"Please call me Madelaine," Dr. Norris said. "Both Marni and Henry told me you were staying with Candy. It's so good of you to do that. I must admit I was also looking forward to meeting you, not only because of Candy, but before this, when Kimberly told me the names of the Soundview partners. Years ago I was at your first showing in the United States. It was about fifteen years ago, Nina. Am I right?" Nina nodded. "Exactly," she said.

"You couldn't possibly know every name who has purchased your work, but I have a Nina Levin on my living room wall The Old Neighborhood Composition Three. That artwork has helped me keep in touch with my beloved childhood—wonderful loving times. It was the first piece I purchased."

Bells and whistles started going off in Nina's head. She knew that she would have a good relationship with this woman.

"Much warm sentiment went into that piece," Nina said. She had given Composition One to her father as a wedding gift. "I'm glad we share similar feelings." If Nina believed in fate, this coincidence would be high on her list. What were the chances that a basis for a relationship was already established between herself and Dr. Norris. "We definitely have an affinity with your artwork and perhaps much more than that," Dr. Norris said. "When Kimberly told me about her new home, I thought it was a very positive situation, and it was. The comradery gave Kimberly the support she needed to help her express personal feelings." Nina thought the same thing. She told this to Marni when she was feeling guilty bringing the three of them together to purchase Soundview. "If only we could have prevented this from happening," Nina said.

"There were many negative forces playing simultaneously. It needed Kimberly, George, and Candy to be in joint therapy. Then it might have been preventable. "Well, now we must see Candy through this. She has spoken of you in our sessions and values the friendship."

"I'm glad," Nina said. "I would like her to come live with me."

"I can appreciate why you want to do this, but Candy has to agree to that idea and then there's the Court's approval." Dr. Norris placed her hand on top of Nina's arm and said gently, "You must also realize, my dear, that you can never replace her mother." Dr. Norris lowered her hand to her side. "But," she continued, "you seem to have good intentions and I get the feeling you'll do what it takes to help Candy put her life together. Your body language tells me that. We'll work together coordinating our efforts and we'll confer each day."

"That will be most helpful, Madelaine." There wasn't much more for Nina to say why she wanted Candy to live with her. She and Madelaine wanted the same thing for Candy, a home with someone who cared. Dr. Norris handed Nina her business card. "Have the lawyer who'll be petitioning the court call me. I'll work with him." Nina tucked the card in her pocketbook. "Thanks," she said. "And thank God for Henry," she said silently. She would have made a complete fool of herself not knowing the legal process.

"You can call me anytime," Dr. Norris said grasping Nina's hand. "See you tomorrow."

Nina slipped quietly into the hospital room, leaned over the bed, and softly kissed Candy's forehead. A faint smile appeared on Candy's lips, and her eyes opened. "You're looking better today," Nina said. "I feel a little better," Candy said softly, "with you here." Nina clasped Candy's hand in hers.

"Dr. Norris visited me," Candy said. "She was here when I opened my eyes." Nina wanting to strengthen the bond between Candy and herself said, "I spoke to her for a few minutes." Candy was silent for a second. "I guess you spoke about me, right? What's going to happen to me?" Candy asked. "I'm all alone." Nina sat on the edge of the bed. "Naturally, we're concerned," she said. Nina moved closer to Candy. "I've been thinking," she said, "would you like to live with me?" She saw Candy's face light up for a second. There was a glimpse of the spirited young woman that she knew a few days ago. "For how long," Candy muttered. Nina leaned over and kissed Candy's forehead. Then she answered, "As long as you want." Nina didn't say anything for a few moments. She wanted Candy to think about what she said. Slowly, she would inform her of the details. "Are you ready to hear more?" Nina asked. Candy nodded. "First," Nina said, "I have to get your consent. Then I petition the court for temporary guardianship. If it all works out, we apply for a permanent guardianship. How's that?" Nina watched Candy take a deep breath. It reminded her of Kimberly. She always did that. "I'd like living with you," Candy said. "Thanks." Nina didn't know what it was like to give birth but hearing Candy's words she knew what it meant to have instant unconditional love for a young person. "I'll get a lawyer moving on it," she said. She leaned down to kiss Candy's cheek but Candy didn't hear her, she had fallen asleep.

Nina sat in her usual chair by the window, her mind busily planning and her fingers busily sketching. Candy's shrilling scream so startled Nina that the pad and pencil slid out of her hands and onto the floor as she stood and went to Candy. Nina soothed Candy by stroking her head and softly saying repeatedly, "It's okay, honey. It's okay."

"I had a bad dream," Candy finally managed to say. "Do you

want tell me about it?" Nina asked taking Candy's hand in her own. Candy nodded. Nina sat on the edge of the bed, close enough to easily hear Candy's soft voice. "There were strangers in uniforms touching my body," she said meekly. "Then Mommy appeared. She looked so pale, like . . . like a ghost. Her eyes were pieces of black coal, and blood dripped out of a large hole in her chest. I tried to stop the bleeding with my hand. I pressed and pressed against her chest." Candy used the hand without an intravenous tube to show Nina how she did it. Then Candy continued. "The blood kept coming through my fingers," Candy whimpered.

"It's okay, sweetie," Nina said. She rocked Candy back and forth careful not to disconnect the IV tube. Nina heard some utterances from Candy. The only word that she made out was father. Releasing her embrace to see Candy's face, Nina said, "What did you say? I didn't hear you."

"My father just stood there," Candy said in a small voice, "watching me try to help Mommy. He had a sick expression on his face. Then he dropped to his knees alongside me asking me to forgive him. When I wouldn't talk to him, he threw me against the floor, smothering me with his body, and begged me to forgive him. Oh, my side hurts," Candy groaned.

Nina thought about what Candy just said and chose her words carefully. She realized that she didn't know George was dead. "It was a big shock to see your mother die in front of you. I've been told by Madelaine and Henry it's normal to relive what happened. It'll help you work out your feelings." Nina caressed Candy's chin and said, "Do you understand what I said? It's okay." Nina was upset that Candy didn't respond to her words but she told herself she must have patience. This isn't going to be worked out quickly.

"He killed my mother," Candy said raising her voice. "Oh, Nina, if I ever see him again, I'll . . . I'll. . . .

"It's normal to be angry but you can't act on it. Look what happens." Very softly Nina added, "Your mother had alot anger also." Candy's eyes became glassy and tears rolled down her cheeks. Nina took a tissue from the nightstand and blotted Candy's face. "Your father had many problems that began when he was a kid and steadily became worse. He didn't know what he was doing, honey."

"My mother is still dead who cares if he did or not. Maybe he'll come after me again?"

"I don't think he will. Candy do you remember what happened? I mean everything."

"How could I forget? I see my father's face and watch my mother die over. Nina, I won't ever forget."

"I know, Candy. But that's all you remember."

"Isn't that enough?"

Nina didn't answer her. She wanted to speak to Madelaine first. "What's important to remember is that your mother and father loved you very much. Unfortunately, their problems made you the victim."

"I should've listened to Mommy. She didn't want me to see Daddy and I let him into the house. It's all my fault." Candy moved her face from side to side. "The pain is really bad," she finally said. Nina thought this wasn't a good time to pursue where the guilt lies. "I'll get the nurse," Nina said.

After Candy was given some medication, Nina stayed at her side holding her hand and waited for the pain to subside. Silently, Nina's mind screamed out her anguish looking at this abandoned child. She thought about another time when she was also filled with such anguish, her mother's death.

Slowly, Nina entered her parents' room. Stale odors of sickness filtered through the air. She saw her mother lying on the bed, her shrunken figure barely visible beneath the covers. A skeleton of the loving person she once was, parchment-like skin drawn tightly across her cheekbones.

"Mama," Nina said, "I'm here, back from Paris." Pops had entered the room behind Nina and held Nina's arm as they approached the bedside. "Nina's here, Sarah," Pops said. He took his wife's frail hand and patted it, then repeated his words.

Nina moved to the other side of the bed and sat down on the chair the nurse had vacated for her. She clasped her mother's spidery hand that had once taught her and guided her. "Mama, it's Nina," she said kissing her sallow cheek. Her mother fluttered her eyelids.

Nina brushed the hair from her mother's forehead and whispered softly, "I love you. I've missed you." Tenderly she held and stroked her mother's hand. Then she began speaking of her life in Paris, meticulously narrating all the events that happened since she had left home. She carefully referred to Professor Pierre Vinot and his wife Michelline as people she met at school. She told her mother that they adopted her into their family. Fortunately, they allowed Nina to stay in their son's apartment in Paris. When she mentioned her teachers saw much promise in her work and she won first prize in a competition, Nina's hand was squeezed by her mother.

Each day that she sat with her mother she watched the flesh become more transparent, the bones more pronounced. She wandered who could believe in a merciful God when such suffering took place. Death could be rationalized more easily if it came quickly, but this . . . this was unforgivable.

For all of Nina's life, time had been a whirlwind. Now, time was nothing more than a torture chamber, forcing her to see, feel, experience happenings of which she wanted no part. She needed this period of her life to be over, finished, ended . . . even if it meant her mother's death.

It was early morning. Nina was sitting on the bed beside her mother holding her hand, listening to her father say his usual morning prayers facing the window. When it came to the Amen, she heard two voices, Pops' and her Mother's. It was the last word that she ever uttered. Soon after, the nurse pronounced her dead. Before Nina pulled the sheet over her mother's face, she said softly, "You still believed, Mama, even after all your suffering. I wish I could." Nina knew Pops heard what she said but offered no words of wisdom. He stood silently at the foot of the bed, eyes pressed closed, tears running down his large sagging cheeks. His prayer book pressed against his heart. Nina and her father sat the required seven-day Shiva period, mourning her mother. Their friends and neighbors, true to the Jewish traditions, wouldn't allow them to be alone. They forced them to talk, to laugh, to eat, and to feel that life was continuing, not only around them, but for them.

"How is Candy now?" Nina felt someone touching her arm.

She opened her eyes. Through her tears, she saw the nurse next to her. "Excuse me," the nurse said, "are you all right?" Nina dabbed the corner of her eyes with a tissue trying to gain her composure. "I'm sorry," Nina said. "I was in another time and place." The nurse smiled at Nina. "Spending time in a hospital," she said, "gives you lots of time to think." How right she was, Nina thought. Her shirt was wet under her arms. "I see Candy is sleeping," Nina said observing the stillness in the bed. "The pain medicine really knocked her out."

"Call me if you need me," the nurse said walking out the door.

"Thanks. I will." Nina glanced at Candy for a moment and decided it was a good time to call Marni. She was ready to petition the court for guardianship. Nina also wanted to speak to Madelaine.

There were issues to be addressed with Candy and she needed the therapist's guidance.

Chapter Twenty-Three

The moment Nina saw Paul enter the hospital room she jumped off Candy's bed. "Hi, Paul," Nina said. "Is something the matter?" She was nervous that the guardianship would not be approved. "No," he answered. "I wanted to tell you and Candy in person, the interview this morning went very well with the court appointed social worker." Nina immediately hugged Candy. "Isn't that good news, honey?" she asked. Candy meekly said, "Yes." Nina's elation went down a few levels by Candy's pathetic response. It was a relief to Nina that her past hadn't caught up with her. She was still considered a responsible citizen. However Candy was going through a frightening time with an unknown future so her reaction was more than understandable. "When does the judge sign off?" Nina asked. Any second wasn't soon enough for her.

"In a few days," Paul said. "Steven Butler will call you here or at home. It's just pushing paper now. That's all."

"Great," Nina said glancing at Candy. "Thanks for arranging everything."

"I can't take the credit," said Paul. "All I did was put Steven Butler in contact with Dr. Norris. They seemed to know their way around family court. Besides this was a special circumstance; the court and the hospital wanted a guardian in place to make decisions for Candy. All interested parties wanted to be accommodating so the judge ordered a social worker to go out immediately."

"Does that mean I can live with Nina now?" Candy asked.

"Yes," said Paul. "She'll be responsible for you but it's only temporary, ninety days. We'll have to go back into court after an updated report by the social worker."

"What do you mean?" Candy asked.

"The social worker will make sure Nina is taking good care of you," Paul said. "I'm confident there won't be a problem."

"We'll do fine," Nina said seeing the concern on Candy's face. "It's all just alot of paperwork. That's what we have lawyers for."

"Well, I've got to go," Paul said. "I'll check with you later. Nina was grateful for his thoughtfulness. "Thanks again, Paul," she said. She appreciated how he handled the matters.

I'm nervous," Candy said. "If the judge doesn't approve, I'll be all alone." Nina overcoming her own doubts said, "That's not going to happen. I'm here for you from now on. You heard what Paul said. The judge is going to sign-off." Nina, to be close to Candy again, sat on the bed. "What about my father?" Candy asked. "You know, what happens to me. They'll take me away from you." Nina wanted to confront Candy's concerns but she and Madelaine decided it was best the therapist tell Candy about her father. "He won't ever harm you," Nina said glancing at the door. She was relieved to see Dr. Norris walk through it. "How do you know?" Candy asked. "Know what?" Dr. Norris asked approaching the bed. "Candy wants to know why she's safe from her father," Nina said clueing Madelaine into their discussion. "Let's talk about it for a few moments," Dr. Norris suggested. "Are you up to it Candy?" Candy nodded. Nina was thankful Candy will finally be told her worst fear, her father, was something she never had to worry about again.

"Let's begin by saying Candy dear, your father loved you and your mother very much," Dr. Norris said.

"I know that for a fact," Nina said. "Your mother called him her prince charming when she first met him. That's very special Candy." How special was it, Nina thought. She didn't believe her own words. All Candy had to do was remember her mother was shot. Nina had the urge to hug Candy and tell her she had enough love to make up for every day she lived already.

"In fact," Dr. Norris began, "your father loved so much that he couldn't live with what he had done." The therapist paused. "He shot himself and died next to your mother." Candy closed her eyes for a second. Nina wandered if Candy was thinking why was this happening to her. "You should have told me this before," Candy said. "I had no idea if you knew or not," Dr. Norris answered. "it was Nina who realized that you didn't know."

"Why didn't he kill me too? It's not fair that I must live with this." Nina rubbed Candy's hand trying to calm her agitation. "Some good has come from your parents' relationship," Nina said. "It's you, Candy." Nina held Candy's hand in her own. "Why me?" Candy said. Nina smiled knowingly and said, "Honey why does anything happen to any one of us. It's called life." Intuitively, Nina realized that was not the appropriate response. This wasn't the time for some philosophical jargon. Candy needed facts to build a foundation for a strong self-image and sense of security. Dr. Norris gave her the needed response. The therapist said, "There are reasons and we're going to explore them." Hopefully, Nina thought, Candy will see it wasn't her fault that her mother and father had a fatal conflict. "She's right, Candy," Nina said. "There are reasons. You and I together will find out what they are with Dr. Norris' help. It's important to understand why things happened. Then you'll have a better chance to control your own destiny." Nina wondered wasn't this a tall order for someone so young and mentally frail as Candy. Didn't it take her fifteen years to get over a love affair? Nina looked from Candy to Madelaine and then inwardly to herself and knew she wouldn't rest until she changed Candy's life around. It was a union for better or for worse.

"I don't have to be afraid of my father anymore?" Candy asked. "He's gone forever," Dr. Norris said.

"It's you and I," Nina said to Candy. With the innocence of a three year old Candy asked, "Nina, you won't leave me?" Those were the words that Nina needed to hear. It gave her the hope that there was a mutual commitment to the relationship. "I promise," Nina said.

Chapter Twenty-Four

Marni closed her apartment door holding an envelope with a copy of the Child Support Agreement that Steven Butler sent over with a messenger. She ripped open the envelope and anxiously reviewed the document. Don had agreed to all of Marni's terms. He would share equally with her the childrens' financial expenses. Steven did his job. How convenient of Don to find the money. She guessed Don wanted the house bad enough.

"What's that?" Greg said. "Sell something?"

"Divorce agreement," Marni said. She felt good that she brought Don around to her way of thinking.

"Oh," Greg said.

"That's how people get divorced," Neil said joining them in the living room.

"This," she said holding the paper in the air, "safeguards your rights. Your father promises to be there for both of you. He wants to share all the bills. He has asked to be able to visit you anytime, but telephone first to see if it's okay. Have sleep over dates. Vacation time. All of this happens if you want to go. It can't interfere with school."

"If we don't want to go," Greg said, "we don't have to?"

"That's right," Marni said stiffening her shoulders. "If you want a relationship with him, you're going to have to work on it."

"Does it say we get our old rooms?" Neil asked.

"He told us that before," Greg answered.

"About phoning," Marni said, "you know all the numbers. Sometimes Barbara might answer at home. She's going to be your father's wife. I predict over time, you and Neil will establish a friendship with her that works."

"Maybe," Greg said. "Well . . . at least you and dad don't have to argue any more and maybe even kill each other."

"Oh, what a thought," Marni said. "Unfortunately, I know why you said that. Greg, Neil let's go into the den and sit." Noticing Neil pick up the remote, Marni said, "Put it down. No television until we talk." Marni sat between her sons on the den sofa. Her arm resting across each of her son's shoulders. "A disagreement," she began, "doesn't lead to violence, that's a whole other thing. Boys, you argue over watching a television program or playing an intendo game. Does that mean you're going to find some kind of weapon and use it?"

"Get real Mom," Greg said.

"No, that's so stupid," Neil muttered.

"Well, your father and I have a responsibility to look after your well being. We would never harm each other. You two," Marni said looking first at Greg and then Neil, "would suffer, with no Mommy or Daddy. We wouldn't do that. We love you. What happened to Candy was terrible but your father and I aren't Kimberly and George. There's the difference. Remember that. It's very important. Divorce is horrible. It breaks up the family but you still have parents, just in separate homes." Marni drew her sons to her, hugging them tightly. She kissed each of their foreheads. "I love you both very much. Being your mother is the best thing in the world."

Hearing the buzzer ring of the apartment door, Marni got up.

"Don't move," she said to her sons. "I'll be right back."

"Hi," Paul said greeting Marni with a light kiss on her cheek.

"I got it," she said closing the door behind him. "Steve sent it over." Marni held up the paper. "Don agreed to everything. Greg, Neil and I are having a discussion in the den. It's really heavy. We're talking about the agreement and about violence and death, Don's and mine." Marni saw Paul grimace for a second. "Let's go and see if we can put some of these fears to rest," he said. Marni returned to the den with Paul. "Greg, Neil," Paul said nodding to each. "What's happening?"

"Greg thinks mommy and daddy are going to kill each other," Neil said. "He's nuts. Real nuts."

"I didn't really say that," Greg said punching Neil in the arm.

"You did so," Neil shouted leaning toward Greg and about to

return the punch. "Boys," Marni said sitting down between them.

"Greg," Paul said, "I think I know where you're coming from. It's a concern with what has happened recently." Paul leaned against the arm of the sofa facing the three of them. "You see that paper Mom's holding, it makes a big difference. Your parents took their disagreements, discussed them with their lawyers and finally came to an agreement. Candy's parents were never able to do that. Now Candy has suffered for it." Marni thought Paul just gave a perfect explanation of rational behavior versus extreme emotional discord and it was so simply said. She thought he deserved to be blessed with a child, hopefully theirs.

"I see what you mean," Greg said to Paul. "Mom said something like that also. It was a stupid thing for me to say."

"It's good to talk about things, honey," Marni said to Greg.

"I want to hear what's on your mind." She squeezed Greg's shoulder then turned to Neil. "Are you clear about this?" she said to her younger son. Marni knew Neil talked about all sorts of things with his friends and with her, too. "I didn't say anything bad," Neil said. If he had something on his mind, he would talk to her. She was comfortable with his response. It was Greg who needed her support and she wanted his approval. His relationship with Don was still on shaky ground. "The agreement is okay, Mom," Greg said kissing her cheek. She was glad he did that.

"Can I watch television now?" Neil asked. Marni wasn't about to let him do that without doing his homework first. She knew that he had no time since he went to a tennis lesson after school. "I just want to watch television for a little while," he said giving her his sweet smile. "Go do your homework," Marni said matching his smile. "If there's time afterward, you can." Neil threw the remote on the sofa. "I better get to the books also," Greg said standing. Marni didn't have to say anything to Greg. He did it on his own. She smoothed her hair behind her ears, watching her sons leave the room. "Kids," she said to Paul, "it ain't easy!"

"At least the divorce will be over soon," Paul said. She knew the agreement was only as good as the person's actions. "Yeah, but will Don live up to his part?" How many times would she have to take him to court for reneging on some term? "Don't worry about something that hasn't happened yet," Paul said. "You're right," Marni moaned. She was annoyed with herself for not enjoying the fruits of her efforts.

Paul moved onto the sofa next to her and she was thankful to slip into his outstretched hands. "How was your day?" he said softly. She snuggled closer to him and said, "Now that you're here, it's better." She put her head on his shoulder. "Just hold me," she murmured but all she could think of was Kimberly. "Why couldn't Kimberly and George put together an agreement?" Marni asked. "If she just tried, she'd probably be alive today. It was tough going for Don and me, but it was worse always in conflict."

"There are many reasons," Paul said, "unfortunately none of them will bring her back. I don't consider her a innocent victim in this tragedy. She had the means to turn her life around once she stepped into Dr. Norris's office. I had the pleasure of working with her and Steven these last few days. She was a strong advocate for a better future for Kimberly and Candy, but she could go just so far. It was up to Kimberly to stop her own self-destruction." Paul kissed Marni. "Enough about that. Let's talk about us. We can move forward now. We'll find out how long until the divorce is official and then we'll set a wedding date."

Marni sat up straight so she could face Paul. "What's the hurry?" She wasn't sure that she wanted to jump into marriage with the ink still wet on the divorce papers. With Kimberly's death, everything seemed more complicated. She loved Paul and wanted to be with him, but she saw a caution sign creep across her gut. "We could wait awhile. What about living together first?" Marni said taking Paul's hand. "We're not kids getting our feet wet for the first time," Paul said removing his hand from Marni's. She pushed a few strands of hair behind her ear. "How about a little while?" Paul's frown bore out what he said next, "I'm not comfortable with that. Besides the clock is also ticking if we want to have a child of our own." Marni knew how to brush that concern away. "I feel good about becoming pregnant," she said, "with all the tests taken during a pregnancy. You know what's growing inside you. That's not an excuse to rush into things."

"I thought you wanted to get married. Has this whole business with Kimberly affected your thinking about our future?"

Marni was silent for a few moments. She really loved him. People lived together to get to know one another. She knew Paul for a long time. Wouldn't it be better to get some normalcy back in her life? Greg and Neil would benefit from it, also. A few times she looked up at Paul and then looked down at the floor. She knew why she was hesitating. Since Kimberly's death, there was a fear of loss. You love someone and then they could be suddenly taken from you. She had a better understanding what Paul must have gone through. She never had to deal with death. Her parents were alive and well and thriving. She never met her grandparents. They died when she was little. What was her fear? She loved him too much. Could she cope with him gone? She felt ridiculous thinking this way. However, it was her reaction to a death resulting from someone close to her suddenly dying. Then there was the guilt. What could she have said to Kimberly? How could she have given her a wake up call to what treasures she held in her grasp? She had Candy, Henry and caring friends. Finally, she had a place to really call a home. Didn't she have the benefits of a successful business? Marni thought for a second maybe she should give herself that wake up call. It was too late for Kimberly but not for her. If she didn't take a chance then she'd be in a living death. Well, Marni Taylor here was your chance. She wasn't afraid of commitment and now it would be with the right man. "Can I wear white?" she said softly bringing Paul's hand to her lips.

"Why not?" Paul answered. "We're marrying each other for the first time. It'll be a small wedding, parents, Greg and Neil, and a few close friends. How does that sound?" he asked. She pictured the wedding outside on the estate grounds overlooking the Long Island Sound. "Perfect," she said. "Do we have to move from here? Oh, it's not important." How could she think of the property at this time? "It's probably not wise to stay here for the kids sake, anyway. What do you think Paul?" She knew that she would consider whatever he said. "I don't think it matters where we live," he said. "It won't wipe out the memory of what happened. It's something we're all going to deal with whether we stay here or move." That was a good point, Marni thought. The memory was carried inside us wherever we go. "Nina and I decided to knock down the guest house. You'll have to obtain for us the permits." Marni moved back to be closer to Paul. "That's a good idea," he said. "We can try it here for awhile. If it's not comfortable, we'll buy something else." Marni allowed Paul to turn her around so her face was near his. He rubbed his nose against the tip of hers. "I know a great real estate broker," he said.

"I love you," Marni said snuggling again into his shoulder. "Everything seems doable with you in my life." Lovingly, she moved his dark hair off his forehead.

Chapter Twenty-Five

Nina sat at one end of her green leather sectional in her living room, Paul at the other. Impatiently, she tapped her foot, watching him open his briefcase and take out the approved petition by the judge, the validation of Candy's guardianship.

"Congratulations," Paul said handing her the document. "You now hold Candy's welfare in your hands." Nina sighed in relief. A lot had gone through her mind the last two days. It was now official.

"Well, Nina," Marni said sitting down next to Paul, "parenthood has arrived for the prominent Ms. Nina Levin. I wish you much happiness, good luck and don't ever forget your sense of humor."

"Are those your words of wisdom?" she asked glancing at the document.

"They are," Marni answered. "Oh, I forgot one thing. Call me anytime. I have a twenty-four-hour advice line."

"I should have called you to pick me up at the hospital," Nina said. "I arrived here only a few minutes before you and Paul. If it wasn't for Henry driving into the hospital parking lot when he did, I'd still be standing there. My car had a dead battery or something."

"More like the starter," Henry said walking in from the kitchen. "The nurse said Candy is sleeping."

"Thanks Henry," Nina said still reading the legal papers.

Everyone remained silent waiting for Nina to finish. It wasn't too long before Nina said, "Everything was in order. Thanks." Now she had to live up to what was written.

"The documents should be accurate," Paul said. "Steven is good."

"I guess Steven Butler could be called a legal whiz," Marni said. "He must have moved mountains to get this all worked out so quickly." Since Marni received her child support agreement, she had a very favorable opinion of him. She was feeling bad about the rough time she gave him. Once the divorce was completed, she was going to give him a gift, a peace offering.

"Sounds like you doubted Steven's expertise?" Paul said. "I guess my assurances didn't count."

"Did I put a chip in your ego?" Marni said. "Sorry about that." Marni tried to give him a comforting smile but she noticed it didn't change his serious expression. "Blind trust is diffucult while in Steven's office changing my world and making sure the kids didn't suffer. What can I say? I'm human."

"Now do you feel better about him?" Paul asked.

"Yes, I do. Thanks for recommending him." Marni was trying to take some sting out of her previous statements.

"What Marni was feeling was normal," Henry said to Paul. "I hear it a lot in my therapy sessions. People are at their most vulnerable point when they go to a divorce lawyer."

"I hope I never know," Paul said closing his briefcase.

"You won't," Marni said. She wanted to reaffirm she's in it forever.

"Paul, some coffee," Nina said. "You deserve a cup." Nina was glad her three favorite people were with her tonight. She had been in touch with the chapel where Kimberly's body was being held for burial. The phone call, like the death of Kimberly, was disturbing for Nina, a reminder of her own mother. However, it was something that she could cope with now in a far better way than in the past. Nina realized that she was truly fortunate to have shared with her mother all her thoughts, her dreams and experiences before she died. She continued to speak with her mother through her art. Each work was the object of her feelings and a monument to her mother's memory. She never forgot it was her mother who first put the paintbrush in her hand. When she was a teenager, she told her mother that she painted for both of them. She now understood what her words meant. Although Nina and her mother had been apart for a few months when Nina was in Paris, they were of one mind at her death. Candy never had that chance. Kimberly was whisked out of Candy's life while she helplessly watched. Nina gave Paul his coffee and then topped off the other cups. "I spoke to the funeral home today," Nina said. "They need someone to make arrangements. I guess as guardian, it's me." Nina looked at Marni soliciting her help.

"Of course, I'll go with you," Marni said.

"Thanks," Nina answered. "Candy is improving. We'll probably have the funeral within a week or so. I just want to put this behind us."

"The funeral is important to Candy's healing," Henry said. "It's all part of the closure process. She'll painfully spill out all her guilty feelings to her mother silently or perhaps verbally but afterwards Candy will feel lighter or perhaps freer. A weight would have been lifted off her shoulders and it'll be easier for her to get on with her life. When my wife died unexpectedly I had regrets that I didn't arrive home soon enough to tell her I loved her. It's normal. At the funeral I made up for that. There are meetings that people can attend to deal with death and loss. Hopefully, Candy will go to one. I lead a few of these discussion groups. They're helpful."

"I went to such a group," Paul said. "It was a catharsis for me. At my wife's funeral I did the same thing as you, Henry, but my words were I'm sorry. That's because I didn't drive her that day."

"My mother's funeral was the saddest time of my life," Nina said. "This may sound callous but I'm going to say it anyway. You can always remarry and start over living happily ever after. A loss of a mother is irreplaceable because there's a bonding from the womb. I light a candle on her birthday and the day she passed on. I visit the cemetery once a year and say a prayer over her grave. For a few minutes, I stand there and tell her what's happening. Before leaving, I put a small rock on the headstone to keep her company. I have much empathy for Candy. She'll miss her mother and I'll miss a friend. The funeral is important to me. I want to say good-bye. In some ways it can be compared to completing a work. My routine is to study the canvas for a day or perhaps a week. My paintbrush is poised to move at any moment. If there are no additions, I go to a new canvas. The preliminary process of Candy moving in with me has been completed. Candy and I are ready to continue our lives together."

"I guess that's what life's all about, end one part to begin another," Marni said. She wandered if she should tell Nina her news. Was this the appropriate time? Nina was concerned about the funeral. Marni decided to keep her marriage a secret. She would wait for the right moment. "How do you feel about me doing a eulogy?" Marni asked. "Personalize the service for Candy. Tell what Soundview meant to the three of us." Marni looked around at the others. She wanted Kimberly's stay on earth to be remembered for something other than a brutal ending. She wanted Candy to have a sense of what her mother meant to others.

"I'm sure Candy would like that," Nina said. Nina was grateful for Marni's suggestion. Nina knew they all had to say goodbye in their own way. Then they would be free to move on. Nina had something to gain from the process. She had someone to nurture and to love. It would fulfill the emptiness that she brought with her to Soundview.

"There's another reason for the eulogy," Marni said. "I brought us together and started our unity. Now I'd like to make peace with the tragedy. Then I'll feel better about setting a date with Paul. We're getting married."

"That's great," Nina said.

"Congratulations," Henry said raising his coffee cup. "Much

good luck and happiness."

"Thanks," Marni said. "I hesitated to tell you, Nina, with all that's going on but I really wanted you to know."

"Well, life does go on," Nina said. "I'm glad you did. When things quiet down, I'll work on your wedding gift. With that news, I believe the sun just burst through the black cloud."

"Well-put Nina," Henry said.

"A Nina Levin original," Marni said, "I love it. Someday I'll have to show Paul your wall."

"What's that all about?" Paul asked.

"You have to see it to appreciate it," Marni answered, then sorry for bringing it up under the circumstances. She glanced at Nina's face and knew she definitely said the wrong thing.

"I don't think now is the appropriate time," Nina said. If Marni was sitting next to her, she would've poured the coffee over her head. "It must've slipped your mind, Marni," she said. "I've reformed. At dinner we discussed this."

"You're right," Marni said. Embarrassed, she didn't think Nina was really serious. She just thought that Nina was tired of Alan. "Oh, the wall is humorous," Marni cajoled, wanting to alleviate any discomfort Nina was feeling. "I think we can all use a little relief. What do you say?"

Nina remained silent. She focused her attention first on Marni, then Paul and finally Henry. Nina wondered what was on Henry's mind. Why did she need Henry's approval? "It's okay," Henry said. His approval supported Nina to act like herself. She always had a sense of humor about her gallery of men. Why should she change now? Henry had become an important part of her life. He made it possible for her to function with some competency regarding Candy's welfare but so did Dr. Norris. However, it seemed that he was doing more than that and she was letting him. She guessed it was until she felt surefooted about herself. Her new self-awareness would help her succeed in the role as guardian. She laughed to herself promising never to forget a sense of humor. It was an important tool for coping with life. "One more time," she said silently. "My studio is upstairs," she declared waving her hand toward the steps. She led the way after flipping on the light switch controlling the studio.

As Henry reached the top step, he said, "Terrific studio." He walked over to a window and looked out. "It's too dark to see anything but don't you face the Sound?"

"Yes, I do," Nina answered. "The landscape is seasonal but I always have the waterview." Nina stood at the end of the gallery of men and watched as Marni, Paul and Henry inspected her canvases. The artwork was filled with bold colors, distorted shapes of ordinary objects found on earth, in the sky or beneath the sea. The abstractions interacted on the canvas giving the illusion of depth and movement. She enjoyed people viewing her work and never tired of the accolades for something she adored doing. "I'll take any one of these paintings for a wedding present," Paul said. "They're all great." She had to give some thought to what she wanted for Marni and Paul. Did she want the painting part of a new group of artwork that she was creating through her brainstorming or one now hanging on her wall? "I'm going to purchase a painting for my home," Herny said. "The question to be answered is which one. May I come back in the daylight to inspect them again? I assume they're for sale," Henry quickly added turning away from the paintings and toward Nina. "We'll work something out," Nina said. The purchase of Nina's artwork instinctively linked her with the collector. Didn't she feel an immediate bonding with Dr. Norris? Her bond to Henry would become stronger.

After awhile, Henry and Paul sauntered over to Nina's gallery of men. They started with Pierre and studied each painting. The farther they progressed along the wall, the more naked Nina felt. It didn't matter to her she was standing fully clothed. By the time Henry and Paul were in front of Alan's portrait, they each had wide grins on their face. "The portraits are too much," Marni said standing between Paul and Henry. "I like your sense of humor, Nina, particularly here," Henry said using his finger to point to the tip of Alan's penis. "For sure, you're not going to get me on this wall." Paul looked closer where Henry's finger was pointing. "Or me," he said.

"There aren't going to be additions," Nina said firmly. "I have decided to store most of the pictures. The ones to remain on the wall will be Pierre the first one and Marty, a young friend of mine in the swim trunks." Paul glanced up and down the wall again. "That's wise," he said. "It wouldn't be smart for a court appointed social worker to see this. They want a protected environment for Candy." Nina quickly chimed in, "And they'll have that."

"Thanks for the levity," Henry said. "It's getting late and I start early in the morning." He walked down the stairs followed by the others. Henry retrieved his coat from the closet. While putting it on, he remarked, "I would be remiss if I didn't say, that was quite a study on the personification of the male."

"I second that," Paul said.

Nina nodded in agreement. "That's exactly what they are," she said.

"Good night," Henry said walking out the door. "I'll be at

the hospital tomorrow, after office hours. If your car is not fixed, I'll give you a lift home."

"Thanks," Nina replied.

"I'll drop you off in the morning," Marni volunteered.

"Okay," Nina said taking Marni's arm. "A few things before you leave. Bonita is going to move Candy's things into the bedroom next to mine." Marni squeezed Nina's arm. "Good idea," Marni said. "What else?"

"Did you hear anything about the guest-house?" Nina asked. "It would be great if we could knock it down before Candy moves in."

"I can answer that," Paul said. "The police are finished with the case. They decided not to interview Candy. The scene spoke for itself. Now, I'm working on a release from the bank. Verbally, they approved it. I'll see if I can hurry them along. A permit has been filled out but I can't pick it up without the bank's written approval. We're in good shape."

"One thing more" said Marni, "Kimberly's place has to be dismantled. When Candy is up to it, let her pick out the things she wants to save. We'll have one big tag sale." Nina knew that was going to be a difficult task for Candy. "Let's give Candy some breathing room," Nina said. "When she's ready, we'll do it together." Nina turned around to glance at her surroundings that she called her home. "I hate to give this all up," she said, "but I might have to. Candy might want to move." A sacrifice Nina knew she would have to make. "See how it goes," Paul said. "I told Marni the same thing. Wherever you move, the memories go with you." That was a truism, Nina thought.

"We're going to live here," Marni said. "Paul is going to move in after we get married."

"After," Nina said. "Very proper."

"Look who's proper," Marni responded, "and changed. Sorry about my indiscretion." Nina shrugged her shoulders. "It's okay," Nina replied. She thought the viewing of her studio went well. Her gallery of men allowed a mystique to surround her. She liked that especially since she was dismantling it for a different lifestyle.

"If there's nothing else, " Marni said, "I'm tired so I'll say good night, babe." Marni leaned over to kiss Nina on the cheek. "Be ready at nine." Nina wondered if between now and tomorrow morning she could wrap and store her portraits and rehang other paintings.

Chapter Twenty-Six

The casket was positioned in the front of the chapel. Its dark wood surface was partially covered by a blanket of white roses. Marni watched from the second row. Kimberly's friends and associates, sadly now her ardent mourners, grieved as they viewed her white silk shrouded body laying peacefully in the open coffin. She sat between Greg and Neil and felt their bodies fidgeting as their arms rubbed against hers. She knew they were extremely uncomfortable, and only too aware of loss, divorce like death, had separated their family, too.

"Marni, they'll be here shortly," Paul whispered in her ear. "I have the chair all set." She knew how difficult this day was for Candy and Nina. Therefore it was important to make sure all the arrangements worked out smoothly. "That's good," she said appreciating all Paul had done. Her eyes followed him until he disappeared through a door. He and Henry had taken over the responsibility of the funeral arrangements. They had been the pillar of strength to Nina and Candy along with Dr. Norris. Marni noticed the therapist had just walked up to the casket. How disappointed she must feel looking at Kimberly. She had tried to help her and in some ways she did. Now Dr. Norris had a second chance with Candy. Marni greeted Dr. Norris with a smile as she sat next to Neil.

People slowly passed by the casket and then found seats. For a few moments the chapel was quiet. Then Marni heard a chorus of hushed voices, "So young," they said. "What a pity." She turned to the side door. Candy in a wheel chair, pushed by Henry entered through the door opening. Nina walked alongside, holding Candy's hand. As they progressed into the room, Henry leaned down and whispered into Candy's ear. She nodded and he patted her on the shoulder. It had been two weeks since the shooting, the funeral services postponed until Candy was physically well enough to attend. The threesome slowly moved across the front of the chapel. The silence within the chapel was broken by a low murmur. Marni listened. "She looks so much like her mother," the voices said. More like twins, Marni thought. A feeling she had every time she was in their presence.

Marni felt poking in her side. "What's the matter?" she said grabbing Neil's hand. "Can I sit next to Greg?" he asked. She saw Paul approaching. "Go ahead," she whispered. "Slide in front of me."

Nina and Henry helped Candy stand up before the coffin. She was holding a single white rose. Nina stood quietly beside Candy, both were dressed in black. "I love you, Mommy," Candy whispered to Kimberly placing the rose across her mother's heart. "I miss you so much." Candy grasped the edge of the coffin. "Forgive me. Please. Please forgive me." Tears trickled down Candy's cheeks. Slowly she bent down and kissed her mother's lips. Nina noticing, a tear remained on Kimberly's cheek and thought it was a gift for evermore. It was now Nina's turn to say farewell to Kimberly. What can you say to a mother whose most precious possession was now in your care. She thought a moment. Silently, she promised to do the best she could for Candy. Nina grasped Candy's hand and with her free hand she brought it to her lips. Then she touched Kimberly's heart. Nina, Henry and Candy stood silently for a while at the side of the coffin. Finally Henry said, "It isn't the dead who suffer. It's those who are left behind." The minister whispered in Nina's ear. The three immediately sat in the first row so the service could begin. Someone squeezed Nina's shoulder. She turned and saw it was Dr. Norris. During these past two weeks Nina had seen the therapist often. She felt that Dr. Norris's efforts had paid off. Candy had begun to understand what caused this day. The therapist devoted to Candy's welfare, continued to make daily visits to Nina's home after Candy returned from the hospital. Nina had participated in these sessions and it gave her a better understanding as to her responsibility. It kept making the bond between Nina and Candy that much stronger.

"Look around," Nina whispered to Candy. "All these people are paying their respects to your mother." Candy quickly glanced behind her and then returned her gaze to the coffin.

"Doesn't Mommy look beautiful?" she said. Too beautiful to be dead, thought Nina. "Yes, she does," Nina said softly. "Your mother is at peace now, honey." Candy shook her head and said, "I want her to be." Nina wished that Candy would achieve peace in her life, also.

"The Lord is my shepherd," the minister began, "I shall not want. . . .

"Want," Marni said silently. She reached for Paul's hand who was now sitting next to her. Marni wanted a long full life with Paul. Silently she prayed, please make it so. The love they shared had suddenly made her world a warmer place to live. Leaning over, she said tenderly, "I love you." He whispered back, "And I love you." Marni's eyes filled with tears of sorrow for Kimberly who would never know the happiness she was going to share with him.

"Yea, though I walk through the valley of the shadow of death, I will fear no evil."

Nina had only half heard the minister's incantations. She was preoccupied with Candy's intermittent crying spells. The word shadow infiltrated her subconsciousness and subtly diverted her attention. "Shadows," she repeated to herself. They were always present when she painted, inciting her creative process. Today, the shadow of death hovered over everyone in this room. She and Candy would live with the shadow of Kimberly and George forever. Nina refused that it hold them hostage, preventing them to move forward. She kissed Candy's hand to share her optimism.

"Surely goodness and mercy shall follow me all the days of my life and I will dwell in the house of the Lord forever."

The minister closed his Bible and took his seat in front of the chapel. Marni stood up, walking with assurance to the podium. Her steps affirmed her belief that she knew who she was. A woman noticed by others. Today she was dressed in a classic black suit. The double-breasted style jacket smoothly draped her slender body. Standing behind the podium, she tucked her hair behind her ears revealing her perfect features.

"Three women," she began, "started living together . . . each of us taking a slice from the other's lives. One's problem became our problem. One's dream became our dreams. One's happiness became our happiness. We shared our inner most thoughts. Our lives were irrevocably entwined, the house called Soundview, became our home. Kimberly and her daughter, Candy, were part of this special family.

Professionally, Kimberly Mathews was a successful architect and entrepreneur. Her respected reputation enabled her to form Mathews Architectural Designs. Many of you who are here today, were her co-workers and her clients. She was a brave person, sweet and good, but not equipped to fight the currents of a crazed society. Yet, she tried to do so anyway." Marni stopped for a moment and looked straight at Candy and said, "You were the most important part of your mother's life. Cherish the good times, accept what is, and go forward."

Marni returned her gaze to the many filled pews. "A foundation, dedicated in Kimberly's name, is being set up under the guidance of Dr. Henry Gordon and Dr. Madelaine Norris. Its main function will be to help women who have been abused or who have been part of a dysfunctional family learn to become independent and resourceful. Your participation is welcomed."

"In conclusion," Marni said, "let us not trod but step lightly. Let us not close our hearts, but open them to understanding and love. Let us not silence our thoughts festering hate and ignorance but open our mouths to debate and dissipate evil. Let us make this our gift to the children, the next generation. We look to the future with optimism. Please join hands and form a chain of unity, the continuum of life." She watched row after row as the people clasped hands. When all arms were linked, she said, "Amen."

Marni left the podium and paused at Kimberly's coffin. She thought, I told you it would take a tragedy to get people moving positively. The pity of it all, it was yours. She walked to Candy, kissed her cheek, and then returned to her seat between Paul and Neil.

When the service was over, Marni stood along with everyone else as Nina, Candy and Henry followed the closed casket laden with flowers out of the chapel. One white rose fell. Nina swooped it up, brushed it against her lips and passed it to Candy.

Marni and Paul flanked by Greg and Neil were the next to leave the chapel. Their arms were firmly linked together. Marni glanced from Paul to Greg to Neil. She made the right decision.

Epilogue

PRESTIGIOUS NORTH SHORE

BE PART OF SOMETHING SPECIAL
MARTAY REAL ESTATE PRESENTS AN ELEGANT HOME. ONE LUXURY RESIDENCE IS OFFERED AT THIS TIME. A TRIPLEX PART OF A MAGNIFICENT MANSION CONVERTED INTO THREE SPECIAL LIVING UNITS. LOCATED ON SIX BEAUTIFUL ACRES OVERLOOKING LONG ISLAND SOUND. POOL, TENNIS COURT AND A BOAT SLIP. ALL AMENITIES. SHOWN BY MS. MARNI TAYLOR. INFORMATION UPON REQUEST. CALL FOR AN APPOINTMENT (226) 684-6886.

About the Author

Writer, entrepreneur, educator, advocate of women's and children's rights for quality of life describe Suzanne Evans. Presently, she is associated with a weekly community newspaper located in upstate New York. Her contributions include human interest stories on community members, contemporary food columns focusing on nutrition and food trends, reviews of local school boards and features on museums and other places of interest. She joined the business world as a real estate professional involved in sales and development of properties on Long Island and Manhattan, New York. She conducted instructional seminars on real estate purchase, financing, and development. Her involvement in the need for quality education led her to become a leader of school organizations and sponsor necessary dialogue between parents and educators. Women issues have always been a priority. She has spearheaded discussion groups and went one-on-one to support, motivate and help women in need. She is a graduate of Syracuse University. Ms. Evans writes and lives amidst the serenity of three-hundred rolling farm acres located in the foothills of the Adirondack Mountains. Continuum is her first novel.